DOMINIC

ALSO BY MARK PRYOR

Hollow Man

The Bookseller

The Crypt Thief

The Blood Promise

The Button Man

The Reluctant Matador

The Paris Librarian

The Sorbonne Affair

DOMINIC
MARK PRYOR

A HOLLOW MAN NOVEL

SEVENTH STREET BOOKS®
AN IMPRINT OF PROMETHEUS BOOKS
59 JOHN GLENN DRIVE • AMHERST, NY 14228
www.seventhstreetbooks.com

Published 2018 by Seventh Street Books®, an imprint of Prometheus Books

Cover image © Shutterstock
Cover design by Jacqueline Nasso Cooke
Cover design © Prometheus Books

Inquiries should be addressed to
Seventh Street Books
59 John Glenn Drive
Amherst, New York 14228
VOICE: 716–691–0133
FAX: 716–691–0137
WWW.SEVENTHSTREETBOOKS.COM

22 21 20 19 18   5 4 3 2 1

Library of Congress Cataloging-in-Publication Data

Names: Pryor, Mark, 1967- author.
Title: Dominic / Mark Pryor.
Description: Amherst, NY : Seventh Street Books, an imprint of Prometheus Books,
  [2018] | Series: A hollow man novel
Identifiers: LCCN 2017034487 (print) | LCCN 2017039330 (ebook) |
  ISBN 9781633883666 (ebook) | ISBN 9781633883659 (softcover)
Subjects: LCSH: Public prosecutors—Fiction. | Conspiracies—Fiction. | Murder—
  Fiction. | BISAC: FICTION / Mystery & Detective / General. | FICTION /
  Suspense. | GSAFD: Suspense fiction. | Mystery fiction.
Classification: LCC PS3616.R976 (ebook) | LCC PS3616.R976 D66 2018 (print) |
  DDC 813/.6—dc23
LC record available at https://lccn.loc.gov/2017034487

Printed in the United States of America

CHAPTER ONE

DOMINIC

The first time I realized my potential for manipulating people was at age eleven, when the headmaster at my prep school handed me a bowl of soup instead of a beating.

A policeman took me to the headmaster's living room nine hours after I'd run away from my private boarding school, a stone mansion in the Highlands of Scotland. It was a frightful place, martialed by incompetent and brutal teachers and stuffed to the rafters with despicable brats, tweed-clad snobs who chattered incessantly about Daddy's chalet in Switzerland or Mummy's new Jag. Fed up with them and the oppressive regime, I'd set off on the five-hundred-mile walk home.

Unfortunately, I turned left out of the driveway instead of right, which itself wound up as a learning moment when it came to planning future escapades.

I made it ten miles before the sun started to set and the wind blowing off the mountains made me second-guess my choice of jacket, shoes, and direction. I've often wondered at the dozen or so cars that sped by me that day, two honking their irritation, one slowing down to stare, and none stopping to inquire if a boy, inappropriately dressed for the climate, might perhaps need help. Maybe the locals recognized my plumage as belonging to Maidstone Hall and were more than happy to let me freeze to death in the wild. If they felt the same way as I did about that school's spoiled, inbred little shits, I wouldn't have blamed them for actively targeting me with their front bumpers.

My six-hour trek ended in the village of Bromstock, where, on the village green, I found a red phone booth. It smelled of polish, which I wasn't expecting. I hadn't been inside many, a few on jaunts to London—and those uniformly smelled of piss and roasted chestnuts, their little square windows coated with stickers advertising all manner of salacious services that I was too young to comprehend. Not this one. Best I could tell, some local busybody had come by and polished each little pane, one by one, before shining up the handset and the rotary dial, which made a gentle rattling sound when I ran my fingertips over it.

At that point I realized another flaw in my plan: no change. I tried dialing my parents' number without paying, as if my own personal emergency would override the mechanics of the phone. It didn't. After hanging up and staring at the black handset for a minute, I realized my options were limited to one: I dialed 999.

The police car was pale blue and driven by a slightly weary and overweight constable whose shirt wouldn't stay tucked in. I was leaning against the phone booth when he arrived, the sun behind me casting sharp light into his eyes that made him squint. I sat in the back seat for the ride to the school, watching the countryside roll past the window, impressed with myself at how far I'd come. Impressed that I'd survived, even, because the lanes looked narrower in the car, the hedges higher, and the trees that lined the roads reached over and extended their black branches as if to pluck us from our route.

"Can you put the lights and siren on?" I asked after a while.

The cop grunted and shook his head. "This isn't a game, laddie."

It took fifteen minutes to get back to Maidstone Hall, and the cop left me in the car as he went to fetch the headmaster. Dumb move on his part, considering I'd just run away from the place, but I was too tired to hop out and hide to prove my point. Plus, I was already fairly sure what the headmaster's reaction was going to be, and I didn't want to make it worse. Something to do with a swishing sound and me not sitting comfortably for a while. I had a cousin at a school not far away—he was a little older but did the same kind of thing, took off without telling anyone, and that was his welcome back.

Turns out I was wrong. The headmaster and his wife, a handsome woman with black hair turning silver, stood in the doorway and beckoned for me to enter. They said almost nothing but followed as the pudgy policeman led me into their living room, where the television was on. A tray table was set up in front of an armchair, and when the cop waddled out, Mrs. Benedict asked if I'd eaten all day. I shook my head. She gestured for me to sit, then left the room with her husband. Five minutes later, he returned alone with a large bowl of soup and some brown bread, which he put in front of me. Then he left without a word.

That bowl of soup told me I'd won. The year of microaggressions I'd committed and gotten away with had gained me little: the fleeting joy of another kid in trouble for something I'd done, a master (it shouldn't surprise you that we called our teachers that) patting his pockets for lost keys or a missing wallet. Each time I ran the risk of being caught, an eleven-year-old powerless to avoid whatever dastardly punishment a master might dream up. And they were vindictive bastards. Once, we were sent on a cross-country run. I puked after about a quarter mile and made it to the matron a minute before the diarrhea hit. She put me in my bed with a glass of water and a pat on the head, but Mr. Dobson, the games master, found out I'd curtailed my run without his permission and made me get out of bed, put on my puke-stained shirt and shorts, and run around the school until I dropped facedown into the mud. A cold shower later,

I was back in bed with a fever and everyone was satisfied that justice had been done. And no doubt assuring themselves that one day I'd appreciate such moments of character building.

But that bowl of soup. That was my punishment for pulling a huge stunt, one the school had never seen before. One that could have killed me and ruined the place forever. They let a boy wander away through the Scottish Highlands, not even realizing for two hours that he was gone, ignorant as to why, and clueless as to how to respond.

My sense of victory was confirmed when the soup was eaten and the movie was over. The rest of the school was doing homework, "prep" we called it, sitting in the six classrooms that surrounded the entrance hall, all of which had windows that looked out over that space. As I crossed it, I heard my own still-wet shoes squeaking on the parquet floor. I walked slowly, and every head lifted from its studies to watch me pass, eyes glued to me, admiration and respect pulsing out from every kid in that school—as demonstrated by the stillness of their writing hands, the silence that swept before me like a royal carpet. No snickers or snide remarks came my way; the little lords and delicate darlings looked up at me as I passed and not down their noses as they were so accustomed to doing. I slid behind my desk three minutes before the end of prep, three minutes pretending to read my history textbook until the bell went.

And I stayed there, tall in my seat as the older boys came to me and asked if I'd be on their team for the table-tennis match they were about to play, asked me if I'd like to kick a football with them tomorrow. I'd won over the entire school with a stupid and poorly thought-out temporary escape. I'd stumped a brutal headmaster and his ice-queen wife; every kid in that school wanted to be my friend; and, although I wasn't to know it then, no teacher would ever lay a hand on me again. Dobson sneered and made his sarcastic remarks, but he had nothing to back it up anymore. Like the others, he didn't dare. Only the school bully, the son of the Earl of Brantley, Matthew MacIntosh, simmered with resentment against me. He was the biggest, toughest, and richest kid in the school, free to push others around while the masters pretended not to see any of it. Free to act like the king he felt he was.

But now I was the untouchable one, sporting a shield of immunity that I'd been handed after one reckless, impulsive act.

Imagine what I could achieve with a little planning.

O

I watched from the back of the courtroom, typing quickly on my computer as I messaged my court chief to ask why my officemate, Brian McNulty, was handling this juvenile's hearing.

I was supposed to be prosecuting this kid, it was *my* case.

Bobby, the sorry little bugger in question, sat at the defense table, wearing his usual hangdog expression and the beige detention pajamas he was so familiar with, and that he'd sported since being picked up for stealing a car in East Austin a week ago.

As I waited for a reply, I channeled my irritation into attention. Specifically on the girl sitting beside Bobby, her hair shining, her face calm and poised, looking as much like the 1950s movie star as she did the first day I saw her in that stunning lime-green dress and heels redder than any man's blood. Her eyes were on Judge Barbara Portnoy, now, and I imagined she was nervous for her brother. Portnoy was lenient on first-timers and occasionally forgiving to second-timers. But she was a baseball umpire on a kid's third strike: *You're outta here!* Appear before her on a fourth or fifth crime, and it was the big house, or at the very least a secure drug or behavioral facility.

Today, though, she was grilling the probation officer who was recommending that Bobby be put on a new probation and start it at Travis County's own treatment center, the Intermediate Sanctions Center, or ISC. It was the last step before juvenile prison itself, a lockdown facility where the kids wore khaki pants, collared shirts, and God-awful sweater-vests. I don't generally view humiliation as an effective method of punishment or rehabilitation, but whoever was selling the county those sweater-vests had apparently made a good case.

At the ISC the kids learned the stuff their parents, those who had any, hadn't taught them. How to tell the time, tie a tie, not spit on the floor. Eat vegetables. At the ISC, the kids spruced up and started learning at the on-site school, got clean of whichever drug was their preference, and after six months were transitioned to the halfway house next door. I'd been a prosecutor in juvie around a year at this point, and, in my experience, once they hit the unlocked halfway house, about a quarter of them snuck out the window on the first night, not to be seen again until their next crime.

That's a long way of saying that I knew full well that fifteen-year-old Bobby had no desire to wear a sweater-vest and, even though I was a prosecutor and not his defense attorney, he and I both knew it was my job to make sure that didn't happen.

My computer pinged quietly, and I read the message from my new court chief, Terri Williams, on our intra-office messenger system.

Brian said you were running late, that he'd be happy to handle the plea deal.

I typed my response: *We didn't have a fucking plea deal.*

A pause. *Please don't swear on messenger, people might see it. It's just not professional.*

Nor is taking one of my cases, which happens to be my concern right now.

Sorry. But why do you care? It's just a car theft with a frequent flier.

I care because I'm a fucking professional.

The cursor blinked, but I knew Terri had given up the fight. For one thing, she needed me: she'd been drafted in from our white-collar division and had no idea what she was doing. Brian McNulty had been at the juvenile division longer, but she was smart enough to know that he was borderline incompetent, so when she needed practical advice or help, she came to me. It's always good to volunteer; it helps build the wall between inquiring minds and my true self.

As for my true self, well, I say that I'm a harmless, musically gifted but empathy-disabled Noussian. I take that from the word *nous* in Greek philosophy, representing mind or intellect. Not that I'm smarter than everyone else, but when you have no soul or spirit, well, there's not much left to go on. That sounds very dramatic; but it's not, and I'm not. The fact is, I'm a lot like everyone else around me. I should be—my personality is my own, but my behavior mimics theirs, and my emotions are based on the way other people express themselves. Just because I don't actually feel those things isn't my fault, and if I don't portray them accurately or appropriately, then it's not for want of trying; and I'm sorry for that failing. Very sorry.

Except, and I'm just being honest here, I don't feel that one, either. It's another failing of mine: a total lack of guilt.

Also, for the record, not my fault.

As for Terri, I actually liked her a lot. A large, black woman with frizzy hair and an even frizzier personality, she'd faced an uphill battle learning her new job, dealing with the politics and person-alities of this place, but she always had a smile on her face and a cheery word. She was one of the most genuine people I'd met at the DA's office, and while that may not sound like a compliment from someone like me, it's meant as one.

I turned my attention back to Bobby. He and his beautiful sister glanced around the large courtroom, and I knew they were looking for me, wondering why I wasn't prosecuting this case and reducing the charge as usual. I was his shield when he came to this place, had handled all three of his previous charges and used the broad prosecutorial discretion of my position to ensure a mix of dismissals, reductions, and gentle wrist slaps. I did this because Bobby and I had a special bond. And I'm not referring to his sister.

No, Bobby was a younger version of me, too young to actually be diagnosed as a psychopath, but headed in the right direction, toward a bevy of psychologists who no doubt had that diagnosis waiting on ice for him. In two years, he'd be old enough to wear the tag that was hung around my neck when I was a teenager in England, old enough to get that stigma permanently stamped on his medical, psychological, and criminal records, an ugly and permanent tattoo that people would be sneering at for the rest of his life.

I'd kept mine hidden in the move to America. No one checked trans-Atlantic records unless there was a reason, and I knew that my BBC accent and charming personality, combined with a University of Texas law degree and burgeoning musical career, raised only interest in potential employers, not red flags. And, as everyone knows, once you're hired by the government, you have to be either a criminal or an utter moron to get fired. My take was that as long as a git like McNulty was able to hang onto his job, I was safe—no matter what suspicions midlevel managers like Terri had.

At the front of the courtroom, Judge Portnoy had paused and was looking my way.

"Our British prosecutor too busy to handle his usual docket?" she said sarcastically. We had a weird relationship, the judge and I. It had started off professional and cordial, but for some reason in the last few months she'd started to poke at me, needle me. To my chief's chagrin, I didn't have the wisdom to sit and take it, but, to Portnoy's credit, she didn't seem to mind me dishing it right back.

"If I were too busy, judge, I wouldn't be sitting here watching Mr. McNulty swipe my cases."

"Then charge him with theft," Portnoy said, before turning back to Bobby. "And young man, I'm glad Mr. McNulty is recommending a secure placement for you. You're a danger to the public and yourself. This is the fourth or fifth time you've been here."

His lawyer, Sarah Muckleroy, leapt to her feet. "Your Honor, he has only two misdemeanor adjudications." Muckles, as I called her, had a target on her back; and it was only because I was still entranced with my own special lady that I'd not zeroed in on her. She was as smart as she was beautiful, and as kind and thoughtful as the Dalai Lama. If I had any kind of decency when it came to women, which I didn't, I would have crossed her off the list forever. She was way, way too good a human being to fall into my clutches.

"Maybe so," Portnoy was saying. "But I'm not talking about adjudications. I've seen this young man's face on considerably more than two occasions, as you well know."

Muckles sat down, and Brian McNulty gave her that smug smile of his.

Portnoy went on. "I'm going to recess the disposition portion of this plea for two weeks. That means you're going home with your sister today on home detention, which means you're allowed to go out with her but not on your own, for any reason. If you set one foot wrong in the next two weeks, you'll spend the next six months here at the ISC—and I mean that literally, as you'll be wearing an ankle monitor. Charge it every day, and do not even think about removing it."

"Yes, ma'am," Bobby said, his head down. I couldn't see his eyes, but I knew the look they held in them: contempt and fury. To his credit, he was learning to play the game, as his voice was meek and respectful. "I'll do right, I'll show that I can."

"I hope so," Portnoy said, then looked at McNulty. "And the State needs to figure out who's handling which cases. I've made it clear in the past, I like continuity in my courtroom." Without waiting for an answer, she stood. "We're adjourned."

"All rise," the bailiff said, and we hauled ourselves to our feet and watched the elegant figure of Judge Barbara Portnoy sweep out of the courtroom.

O

McNulty huffed his way into our shared office, not meeting my eye.

"What the fuck was that?" I asked mildly.

"I thought you asked me to handle it if you were late." His brow furrowed, as if he really thought that. "A couple of days ago."

"Bullshit."

"Well, you *were* late; I was covering for you." He probably heard the whine in his own voice, so he looked up and said more assertively, "You're welcome."

I held his eye. "Don't handle my cases without asking me. Understood?"

"What's the big deal, Dom? Seriously? Another little shit steals another friggin' car, so what do you care?"

"You heard the judge; she likes continuity with the cases in her court."

"Since when did you care what she wants?" McNulty snapped. "Or anyone else?"

Terri Williams appeared in the doorway. "There a problem, guys?"

"No," I said. "Just friendly banter. You know how we are." I gave her my most innocent smile.

"That's why I asked," she said. "Anyway, you fellas have a minute?"

"Sure." McNulty dropped his plump form into his chair. "What's up?"

She lounged against the doorway and gave us a broad smile. "A fun opportunity for one of you."

"Hey, I don't volunteer," McNulty said quickly. "I got a lot on my plate already."

"You haven't heard what it is yet," Williams said sweetly. "And when you do, I'm guessing you'll change your tune. But looks like you get first dibs, Dominic."

"Fire away," I said.

"As you may know, the DA's office hasn't always had the best relationship with the Austin Police Department," she began.

McNulty snorted. "Because they do crappy investigations and their offense reports are usually incoherent?"

"That's a long word for you, Brian," I said.

"Hush, both of you," Terri said. "From their perspective, they do a ton of work, write all these reports, and then we dismiss cases without consulting them. Or even letting them know." She held up a quieting hand, to McNulty not me. "I'm just telling you what their perspective is."

"Fine," McNulty said. "So, what now—we have to consult with them on every case?"

"Nothing like that," Terri said. "We have a new liaison program in place. You already know that APD divides Austin into nine sectors for patrols. Each sector will now have a prosecutor assigned to it. The day shifts will have your cell number in case they have legal questions and, here's the best part, a couple of times a month you'll ride out with a Thursday evening or night shift, and get the next day off."

"Wait," McNulty said. I could see the wheels turning in his mind. "So I can work Monday through Thursday, then ride out Thursday night and have Friday off."

"Right," Terri said. "Except I think Dominic gets dibs, since you wanted nothing to do with this."

"I was totally kidding," McNulty said. "Come on, seniority wins, surely."

"Sure it does," I said. "On the county scale, I'm a level six attorney; you're a level five attorney. I win. When do I start?"

"No, I meant seniority down here. I've been down here the longest, I should have the choice."

Unfortunately, he was right and I knew it, that's how this place usually worked. "Why can't we both do it, get different sectors?" I asked.

"Yeah, or that," McNulty agreed.

Williams shook her head. "Sorry, I checked already. They only want one from juvenile. Each trial court will have someone assigned, as well."

McNulty turned to me, his voice high and a little desperate. "Don't you play gigs on Thursday nights?"

"Sometimes," I conceded. "But I can probably move them to Fridays. Wednesdays if I have to."

"Much as it pains me, I should probably stick with the house rule," Williams said. "Sorry, Dom, that gives Brian right of first refusal."

"And he already refused," I said.

"He got pretty close to it, I agree." She wagged a finger at McNulty. "Next time, be more of a team player else I *will* bypass you."

McNulty ignored the chastisement. "When do I start? Any training or anything to do?"

"No, but there are some rules," she said. "You wear a jacket or polo shirt with the DA logo on it."

"Can I carry?"

"No guns; absolutely not."

"What about a bulletproof vest?"

"You realize you're gonna be sitting in a car all night, not getting in gunfights, right?" I said.

"If you want a vest, you're welcome to buy one," Terri said. "As far as I know, APD doesn't provide them to riders, and we don't either."

"Cool," McNulty said. "I'll check online, see how much they are."

I could just see him, lacing up combat boots, strapping himself into the heaviest vest he could find, boning up on the lingo. He'd probably strap a fake .32 to his ankle and hope no one noticed, probably start crying if they did.

Terri handed him a piece of paper. "These are the sergeants for the evening shifts this Thursday, one runs from two p.m. to midnight, the other from four p.m. to two a.m. Choose one, e-mail the sergeant to arrange pickup from here, and do at least six hours."

"And I won't see you Friday." McNulty grinned and picked up his cell phone. "Better let the girlfriend know. Excuse me."

He left the office, no doubt headed out of the building so he could crow to his vapid girlfriend about how cool he was now, riding out with the cops every week, but doing it out of earshot of anyone who knew what a dick he was. Which happened to be everyone in the building.

"I thought this was a liaison program," I said to Terri. "You really want that idiot being the face of the DA's office?"

"Be nice, Dom. Look on the bright side: he won't be here to annoy you on Fridays."

"Now to take care of the other four days of the week," I said with a smile.

She looked at me, and for a second I was afraid she'd taken me seriously. But then she checked the hallway was empty and said, "There's one other thing."

"One good thing or bad thing?"

"That depends, as always."

"I get to go back to trial court?" In truth, I didn't mind juvie, it wasn't as bad as I thought it'd be. But I missed trying the big cases, the murders and rapes and robberies. I liked the performance of jury trials, which we never had in juvenile, and I liked seeing my name in the newspaper every month or two. I'd told Terri when she arrived that I wanted out, that if she had a chance to advocate for my return, I'd like her to. She was cool about it, understood completely, and I actually believed her when she said she would.

"Not that, no. Sorry." She gave a deprecating smile. "I have brought it up, I promise. No, it's about Brian, actually."

"Terri, I swear to God, if they move that useless, lazy sack of—"

Again she held up a calming hand. "No, don't worry about that. Thing is, Judge Galaviz is retiring in a couple of weeks."

"Oh really? That's a little sudden, isn't it?"

"I was talking to her the other day. She went to one of those retirement seminars the county puts on from time to time and realized she's eligible before she thought she was. Her husband has a good job so, as she put it, why hang around here longer than necessary?"

"Fair enough," I said. Michelle Galaviz was an assistant public defender years back and had been appointed to her current position about nine years ago. Barbara Portnoy was the only elected district court judge; the other three in juvie were, technically, juvenile referees or associate judges. It was a county job like any other;

you applied, got interviewed, and whoever had the most contacts with the deciding committee got the job. Which meant a nice salary bump, an office with a window, and a couple of black robes. Not to mention power over the lives of several hundred kids a year.

And as that thought went through my head, I knew a couple of things—one of them being what Terri was about to say.

CHAPTER TWO

BRIAN

When I got back to my office, Dominic was watching me with that look he has. I've tried to explain it to my girlfriend, Connie, but she doesn't get it. It's a cross between looking right through you, and seeing everything you're thinking. I don't like it. I expect it's a cultural thing, him being British. Well, English, to be precise. He gets pretty annoyed when you say *British*, and so I do it sometimes for kicks, but he doesn't mind.

We get on pretty well, actually; we're both big into music, though I'm more of a listener than a player. And he's really good. I've been to half a dozen of his shows. He acts like a bad-ass at work sometimes, but when he strums that dang guitar and sings with his low, melodic voice, man, you can see the female population of any bar just swoon. Some of the guys, too, if I'm honest. This is Austin, after all, where anything goes. The weirder the better. Not that being gay is weird—I'm not saying that at all.

Anyway, Dominic's nice enough. Gives me grief sometimes, sure, but from what I can tell, he does that to people he likes. And, of course, I give it right back.

I sat in my chair and gave him a cheery smile. "So, what should I do with my Fridays off?"

"I can make several suggestions, if you like."

"Connie was pretty happy."

"That you'll be out on Thursday evenings? Maybe I'll pop over and keep her company."

I laughed. "She'd probably like that, you English bastard. She was pretty impressed last week." It was the first of his gigs she'd seen, and "impressed" was me playing it down. I actually got a little annoyed, how much she went on about how awesome he was. I mean, it's fine to have a little crush or whatever, but keep it to yourself. Especially when it's on a friend and colleague.

"Remind me which trailer park you live in."

"The one without Mexicans," I joked. "Oh, wait, no such thing."

"So I gather you might not be doing this ride-out thing for long."

The change of subject, and his tone, threw me just for a moment; then I figured Terri Williams must have told him my news. Potential news.

"Yeah, so I was going to tell you myself," I said. "They posted the associate judge job last Friday, and as soon as I told Connie, she pushed me to apply right away. I mean, I would have anyway, as I did before. But Connie, you know, she loves the idea of me in a robe. And Judge Tresha Barger suggested I apply, too, and since she's on the appointment committee, I figured that was a good sign."

Tresha was sort of an old friend, having worked at the DA's office in trial court with me, even though I wasn't there long. Then she went to do some CPS-related job and so we saw each other a lot at juvie. She was appointed to the bench about four years ago. It's hard to be friends with a judge, Judge Portnoy thinks it looks bad for judges and lawyers to hang out, but Tresha and I get along and, I think, would like me on the bench with her.

"Maybe I should apply, too," Dominic said.

I couldn't tell whether he meant it. "You can if you want. Applications are open for another week, I think. Although, like I said, Judge Barger's on the committee." *And we both know she doesn't like you much.*

"Good point," Dominic said. "I like this gig well enough. Maybe I'll get to ride out with the cops and eventually go back to trying real cases."

"Yeah, true." I decided to mess with him a little more. "Although, in the meantime, maybe you can be assigned to my courtroom. Give me a chance to boss you around in front of everyone."

"You'd like that, wouldn't you?"

"Have you call me 'Judge McNulty,' and 'Your Honor.' Stand up whenever I come into the room."

"Can't wait."

"Hold you in contempt, too, if I have to."

"It'd be mutual, at least."

"Hey, don't think I wouldn't if you were disrespectful."

"You know, Brian, there's a pretty good chance of that."

"Yeah, I think I would like being a judge," I said. "Quite a lot."

"This is America; anything's possible." Dominic stood up. "I'm headed to Starbucks, want anything?"

"No, I'm good; thanks, mate." He looked at me like he always does when I call him "mate," a mixture of amusement and something else, probably exasperation. I kind of wanted to tell him that I really *would* like him in my court if I became a judge. He's always the smartest guy in the room, knows how to make a decision, and is very fair to the kids. More lenient than I am as a prosecutor, that's for sure, but I don't have a problem with that. We all have the same mission; the DA's office, the probation department, the public defender's office, and the judges: *fix* the kids, don't punish them. Sometimes I lose patience with the repeat offenders and want to hammer them, a bit like Judge Portnoy does, but Dom always seems to have that extra bit of patience.

A good example is something he started doing about three months ago. It raised some eyebrows at first, but now it's all cool.

You see, there's always been this impassable barrier between prosecutors and defendants. On a good day they'll nod at each other in court, but any communication between them is forbidden, unacceptable. Unless, of course, a defendant testifies in court, which we prosecutors love, because then we get to cross-examine them. But otherwise, no communication at all, ever. Except, Dom went to the chief public defender and suggested they try exactly that. He pointed out that everyone had the same goal, and both sides could benefit. First, if the ADAs started talking directly to these kids and seeing them as more than just hooligans, they'd likely be more lenient, more inclined to try this program or that placement rather than arguing for lockup. And he argued that the DA's office would benefit because it'd be easier to figure out who the real bad apples were and who could be saved. He even drafted a written contract that both parties would sign, saying nothing from those meetings could be used in court.

All seven public defenders were pretty surprised, but he was persuasive and they let him do it on a few, select clients. The super good ones, of course, who'd made one mistake and were otherwise perfectly normal kids. Well, except for that one kid, Bobby someone. Give Dominic credit, he seemed to connect with that kid and tried real hard to talk some sense into him. Bottom line is, it worked for both sides and we all started doing it. I don't like to very much, as I find it hard to talk to them. I mean, it's my problem, I know, but even so. And since I applied for the judge job, I had to stop because I won't be able to preside over the cases of the few I did talk to. But all that's to say kudos to Dominic for starting this. And to the public defender's office for being open to it.

Of course, with the kind of joking, semicompetitive relationship Dominic and I have, I can't very well tell him all this. Maybe when I'm a judge I can be more open and up-front. We'll see.

CHAPTER THREE

DOMINIC

It was either coffee or strangle the smug little weasel. I was pretty confident that if it came down to it, Terri Williams was an astute enough boss to keep me out of Judge McNulty's court as best she could. But in reality, with vacation schedules and people being out sick, if that tosser became a judge, I'd have to appear in front of him now and again.

The nearest Starbucks was a five-minute drive, and I took the time to call my special lady.

"Hey, Dominic," she said. "What happened back there in court? Why was McNulty handling Bobby's case?"

"Yeah, sorry. I have no idea why he jumped on it like that."

"Is Bobby going to be sent to the ISC?" She sounded genuinely worried for him.

"We'll see. Any chance he can behave himself for the next two weeks?"

"Like not commit any crimes?"

"That'd be a start," I said. "If he stays out of trouble, goes to school, reports to his probation officer, all that crap, then I can probably keep him out."

"For two whole weeks?"

"Yep. And make sure he keeps that monitor charged."

"I'll do what I can." She paused. "So, are we still on for tonight?"

"We are; I'll be there at six."

I'd planned a surprise birthday party for Bobby, not exactly a sweet sixteen, but somewhere in that general vicinity. I wondered if he'd find it as amusing as I did, a man without an altruistic bone in his body planning a surprise for a kid who couldn't care less, about his age, surprises, or nice gestures.

But one of my roles was to show him how to live with his condition. Our condition. And I planned to explain to him that making pointless gestures and going out of your way to make people feel good was a part of other people's lives, and needed to be a part of his. Accepting altruistic offerings with gratitude, albeit faked, was also a part of life.

I managed to stay out of Brian's way the rest of the afternoon, mostly by plugging in my earphones and pretending not to notice his attempts at conversation. By the time five o'clock rolled around, he packed up to go home, and so I ignored his cheery little exit wave, too.

I got to my lady's house just before six, still in my suit, only to find the surprise aspect of the party was ruined. Bobby was nowhere in sight, but I could hear the shower going in the one bathroom.

"I couldn't get him to leave the house," she said matter-of-factly. "Also, two of his friends flaked and one got picked up on a warrant."

"He really needs to get new friends."

She threw me a *No shit* look.

I said, "Just us, then?"

"Happily families," she said with a smile. "I'll go out and get pizza. You can try lecturing him on how to behave for the next couple of weeks."

"Maybe I'll teach him the word *fortnight* while I'm at it."

"Seriously, talk to him." She handed me a beer, and I sat on the couch.

"Oh, I will." I looked at the beer can. "I have to open this myself?"

"Use your razor-sharp wit." She picked up her bag, held her hand out for my car keys, and then went out of the front door. I sat and waited for Bobby to appear. A couple of minutes after the water cut off, he opened the door and walked into the small living room, wearing a towel around his waist. He didn't say anything, just looked at the beer in my hand and went into the kitchen.

When I first saw him about a year ago, he'd looked like a kid, and I was taken aback by how much he'd changed in just twelve months. He had that teenage body now, pale skin over taut, thin, muscles, hairless and a little awkward in himself physically. Unlike a lot of his cohorts, he had no tattoos, which I put down to his sister's influence combined with his lack of allegiance to any other person, place, group, or dumb symbol. He started to leave the kitchen with a beer.

"Dude, put that away."

"Fuck you."

"Seriously, your PO can show up anytime and test you. If you want to get locked up, drink away, but I told your sister I'd try and stop that happening."

"Then where the fuck were you this morning?"

"Five minutes late."

"Yeah, and look what happened. Thanks a lot."

"Oh, really?" I raised an eyebrow. The left one, I can't do my right. "The kid who steals things is going to lecture someone for being five minutes late?"

"I'm not lecturing," Bobby said. "I'm saying that you being late is the reason I'm looking at being locked up."

"Yeah, so I think I'd be more inclined to put that down to you stealing the car."

He gave me a sneer. "I was gonna give it back."

I nodded at the beer in his hand and he swore under his breath and put it back in the fridge.

"Just two weeks. Keep your shit together and that monitor charged for two weeks, and I'll do my best to have you serve your probation at home."

"Two weeks, shit." He pointed to his ankle monitor. "This fucking thing is gonna give me away."

"Behave yourself, and it doesn't matter what that thing says."

"There must be a way to get it off without anyone knowing."

I smiled. Two weeks was a long time in his world, a reality I had to acknowledge. "Funny you should mention that. Got any olive oil?"

"No clue. You serious?"

"Very. The PO who put that on happens to be addicted to pain pills, and was very grateful when I gave him a handful. I'm guessing it's not on too tight, and with a little oil you can slip it right off."

"On fleek, bro, I'm gonna try now." He went into the kitchen and rummaged through several cupboards before finding a bottle of olive oil. "Extra virgin," he snickered. He sat at the round table that separated the kitchen and living area, and smeared oil over his ankle and the monitor. With a little grunting and not much effort the device was off and in his hand, triumph in his eyes. Then they clouded—people like him, and me, rarely do favors for people without an agenda, and he knew that better than anyone.

"So why would you do that?" he asked.

"Because I'm trying to help you. I figured you wouldn't stay home, so this way you don't have to."

"But now the PO knows, has something on you."

"No, he doesn't. When would it ever be in his interest to say anything? Even if he did, I can deny the conversation happened and, when it comes down to it, he's the one who put it on too loosely, not me."

"Yeah, maybe."

"Do me a favor, though. POs make unannounced visits, so stay home as much as you can, and while you're here keep that thing on your leg. That way you won't lose it or get caught out. Seriously, if you have to leave the house, then for fuck's sake don't forget to break out the olive oil, but otherwise don't."

Bobby nodded. "Makes sense."

We looked at each other for a moment, trying to figure out where we were. Normally we read other people like this, a look in the eyes, a facial expression. But Bobby and I doing this to each other, well, it's like facing a couple of mirrors together. A whole lot of blank.

Eventually, he spoke. "Look, so I don't owe you any favors, I got some info you might want."

"Oh yeah? Terrorist plot? Winner of the next Kentucky Derby?"

"Better. You remember that cop called Ledsome?"

Oh, yes. She'd investigated a robbery and murder about a year ago, one my roommate masterminded and tried to blame on me. She was a smart cookie for sure; and, without actually figuring it out, she'd indicated that she knew I wasn't quite all there. I'd tried, in several subtle ways, to seduce her, but she'd never given me an inch.

"What about her?" I asked.

"She came to see me. While I was locked up."

A coldness settled around my chest. "Why?"

"Asking about you. That murder."

"Bullshit. Why would she ask you about me?"

"She was asking several kids. Maybe she knows you're banging my sister."

"No one knows the three of us are connected," I said. I could play it down all I liked, but we'd worked very hard indeed to make sure our friendship remained a secret. We didn't talk when she came to court, we didn't meet up in the parking lot, and we even avoided eye contact. "What did Ledsome ask you?"

"Not much. Once she started asking about my sister, I told her to fuck off."

"Those should've been your first words to her," I said.

"I wanted to know if she was trying to implicate me in anything."

"It's a closed case; the perp's in prison."

"Shit, Dom, you really say 'perp'?"

"Bobby. This could be serious. If she thinks I'm involved—"

"Or me," he said. "She could fuck both of us if she wanted."

"There's nothing she can do. Just don't talk to her, I'm surprised your attorney let her do that."

"She told him it wasn't about my current case, and that it could only help me."

"And here you are, looking at being locked up. Real helpful."

"No shit." He chewed his lip for a moment. "You know what I could do."

"Yes. You could not talk to her, or any other cop."

"No, man. Take her out."

"For dinner?"

"Stop being a prick."

I lost my cool then. I wasn't helping this kid out of the goodness of my heart; I was doing it for his sister and so he wouldn't get *me* in trouble. But this kind of talk, if it turned into anything, was going to land both of us in prison. I sat forward on the couch.

"Listen to me. Sooner or later you're going to turn seventeen and realize that you can't game the system anymore. You're smart, but the adult system doesn't give a shit. Either that, or you're going to do something so fucking stupid that I can't help you. That no one can help you. Stealing cars and smoking weed is chickenshit, Bobby, but when you start saying stuff like that, it makes me very, very nervous."

"You're not my fucking dad."

"And even if I was, so what? I never listened to mine, and neither would you." He didn't say anything, so I carried on. "Look, I don't mean to lecture you, I really don't. But you have to understand that as smart and ruthless as you think you are, sometimes it's not enough. You so much as look at a cop the wrong way, all hell breaks loose."

"You've done it." *It.*

"I'm going to assume you were kidding about taking out a cop, Bobby, I mean it. You do that and the FBI, the Texas Rangers, and every patrol officer, desk sergeant, and prison guard in the state will be gunning for you."

"I know that," Bobby snapped. "But what if she *does* connect you to that heist? Or thinks she can? What if she thinks I have something to do with it? I'm just supposed to sit here and catch a case? A fucking murder case?"

"She's got nothing on us, because we didn't do anything. Maybe she's just making sure; I don't know. But one thing I can promise is that the best way to catch a murder case is by killing a cop. You know who gets away with that?"

"Who?" he said, almost sulkily.

"No one. No one gets away with killing a cop. Ever."

"First time for everything."

Smart arse. "Yeah, OK. So, how're you going to do it? Arsenic in her martini? Missile from a drone? Or will you shoot her with a gun that the cops can trace back to you, using bullets that'll be linked to you, in a public place that probably has cameras and eyewitnesses?"

"You think I'm too stupid to do it?" His face flushed with anger. "You don't tell me what to do. No one does, not even my sister."

Like me at that age, he was impulsive, hated being lectured, and was convinced he was always right. He'd need to learn from his own mistakes. They were the best lessons, but if one of those mistakes was murder . . . well, there's not much coming back from that if you're busted. And this wasn't just about saving his arse, but mine as well. If he did something as nuts as killing Detective Ledsome, someone would either know or figure out that she was asking questions about me—and those questions would start being asked by FBI agents, and a lot more pointedly. I had to make him understand that.

I softened my tone, backed away from the confrontation. "You're definitely not too stupid, Bobby. I'm sure you could do it and get away with it for a while. But that's my point. It's a matter of pride for them—they don't care if you shoot some drug dealer or gangbanger on East Seventh. Sure, they'll look into it, make a show of it, but if it goes unsolved for a couple of months, then hey-ho and they're on to the next one. But when a cop gets shot, there's no brake applied, *ever*. You don't need that kind of heat no matter how smart you are. Even if you get away with it, you'll always be looking over your shoulder."

"Kinda like we are now." He was sulky again, but at least not hostile.

I smiled. "Nothing like we are now. Right now a cop has a bug up her arse and is chasing ghosts. She'll either hit a brick wall or get bored or busy and find something else to do. We just need to sit tight until she buggers off."

"Buggers off," he mimicked. "She fucking better." He got up and pulled the towel from his waist, walking naked in front of me to his bedroom. It was the kind of power move I've made a dozen times, going for shock value, sexual intimidation. He should've known it wouldn't work on me, of all people.

Just like I should've known that he, of all people, wouldn't listen to my advice.

CHAPTER FOUR

BRIAN

I felt self-conscious in my ride-out gear, to be honest. The polo shirt was a little tight and I thought it kinda made me look like I had boobs. But Dominic said it made me look official, like when we encountered members of the public, they'd think I was in charge. And the cop I rode with was cool, too. Fernando Chipelo. His family was from Portugal, but he'd grown up here, so he spoke like an American.

He explained how it worked, said he'd had riders before. I was supposed to stay in the car until he said it was OK to step out, which made sense. Dominic had ridden out quite a few times, just because he liked to; and he said he always got out with the cop, unless it was a traffic stop, so I guess either he violated protocol or was lying. Knowing him, I'd guess the former.

The coolest thing was when he showed me the button that released his semiautomatic rifle, an AR-15. He said it with a smile, like there's no way I'd have to use it, but it got me wondering. And he showed me the little red button that would have every cop in Austin racing to help us. Those were good things to know. I mean, if things went badly, I'd be able to help one way or another, which is important.

He also showed me the computer that sat between us. Touch-screen, and it had all kinds of capabilities. Mostly he used it to show what calls were active, but it also had a map of Austin and could give directions to the incident we were going to.

Things were quiet to begin with and we cruised around his favorite parts of the sector, the suburban southwest of the city. At around six we were dispatched to our first call, a car crash, no injuries. Someone had run a stop sign on Convict Hill Road, and the caller said he was trying to blame the old lady he hit, or so the caller claimed.

We pulled up behind both cars, and I thought I recognized one of them, but I couldn't place it. I looked through the windshield as Chipelo approached the driver's side of that car, the male's, the one at fault. He took the guy's driver's license, but instead of coming back to the patrol car, he kept looking at me, nodding and then smiling.

Then the door opened and Dominic stepped out.

He gave me a wave and started filling out paperwork for the accident while Chipelo spoke to the older woman. I got out and wandered over to Dom.

"What happened, man?" I asked.

"I wasn't paying attention, drifted through the intersection and clipped her."

"You're not hurt or anything?"

"No, and I think she's OK, too. I checked, but she was pretty steamed."

"Yeah, well, can't really blame her." I inspected the front of his car. "Can you drive it?"

"Should think so. I just need to finish this paperwork and see if your cop's giving me a ticket."

"He's supposed to if it was your fault."

Dominic winked. "Ah, but I didn't tell him what I told you."

"You lied?"

"No, of course not. I just withheld incriminating information, as is my constitutional right. You've heard of the fifth amendment, I'm sure."

"Yes, of course."

"Exactly. And you're not gonna say anything, are you?"

He cleared his throat and gave me one of those looks. I answered back, "Me? No. I didn't see anything—wasn't here when the accident happened."

"Good man." He glanced up as Chipelo approached.

"Both cars are drivable, everyone's OK, and I can't assess fault," the officer said. "If there's nothing else I can do for you, we'll head out."

Dominic reached for his phone. "I'm good. Just make sure you take care of my office-mate here. If there's one person liable to get himself shot, it's Brian."

Back in the car, we looked at the computer. A new call had come in, and Chipelo was reading the text. I couldn't decipher most of it, the dispatcher used a lot of shorthand terms. He saw I was having trouble and translated.

"Suspected burglary of a residence. Not clear who the complainant is, but the homeowner is supposed to be on vacation. Probably a neighbor who called it in." He put a hand to his earpiece. "Hang on. We have to go, upgraded to hotshot, the bad guy is still in the house and we're closer than anyone else. Strap in."

He reached up and pressed the buttons for the overhead lights and siren, and pulled a screeching U-turn, the Crown Vic rattling and roaring as we sped toward the Legend Oaks neighborhood. I glanced at the map and saw how close we were, Chipelo slowing only when we got to the lights at Escarpment and Convict Hill, traffic stopping for him as the siren screamed. He hit eighty along the wide Escarpment Boulevard, then turned right up a hill, I didn't see the street name.

He killed the siren but kept the lights going. "If there's someone in the house," he explained, "we don't want to let them know we're coming."

Adrenaline surged through me at the thought of us coming up on one or more people sneaking through someone else's home. I hoped Chipelo didn't see how pale I'd gone—I get carsick at the best of times, and this was making me more than queasy. Luckily for me, we were close to the cul-de-sac. Chipelo parked across the entrance, a couple of houses away from the target address, and killed the overhead lights.

"Looks like the front door is open," he said. He poked at the screen, bringing up the map. "De Jong is about a minute out; he has a rookie with him. We'll go in when they get here."

"You want me to stay in the car?"

"Definitely." He glanced in the mirror and touched a button on his body camera. "I'll get in trouble if this isn't on. It connects straight to the Arbitrator video recording system, so you can watch live on my computer what we're doing."

"OK, cool. I won't move until you say it's clear."

He nodded and got out of the car to confer with his buddies who'd just arrived. I alternated between watching the body-cam footage and looking out the window as they moved toward the house. It looked like they sent the rookie around back, judging from his uncertain movements. As Chipelo and his colleague De Jong got close to the door, they drew their weapons, and my heart beat faster. I took off my seatbelt in case I needed to duck out of the car, and looked at the button on the control panel that released the AR. What had seemed like a cool possibility an hour ago now seemed like a disaster waiting to happen. In fact, as those guys went through the front door, I knew for sure that I had neither the training nor the courage to use a gun anywhere but the range.

As they disappeared inside, I stared at the screen. The image went dark but then adjusted, and Chipelo was calling out, "Austin Police, Austin Police, anyone home?" But I also heard music and De Jong saying something about upstairs. A moment later I could see the stairs, winding up and to the left, and every now and again Chipelo's gun would swing into view as he cleared left and right.

The top step came into view, then a small landing and a closed door. I assumed it was a bedroom door. I was spellbound, eyes glued to the screen as Chipelo's hand reached out and rested on the door knob.

"On three," he whispered to De Jong, the music now turned off, and I counted along in my head.

One. Two. Three.

In one swift moment they went in side by side, and right before my eyes the narrow doorway opened into a large bedroom. The camera jostled and bounced with Chipelo's movement but then went still, and there was no mistaking the brief flash of a naked woman leaping up from the bed and streaking toward an open door that I presumed to be the en suite bathroom.

There was no mistaking what was going on, either: I saw another woman, older, each appendage tied to a bedpost, with headphones clamped over her ears and a ball-gag in her mouth. Her head and shoulders were propped up on pillows, and her eyes bulged with what must have been shame, or possibly rage, her face crimson as she strained at her bonds.

Chipelo and De Jong must have stopped and stared, too, because the whole scene froze, almost deathly quiet, apart from some animal sounds coming from the furious woman on the bed, who finally managed to spit out the gag, a line of drool falling across her chin.

At that point, my mouth quite literally fell open and I spoke aloud to myself, not caring whether the patrol car's recording equipment caught my unofficial identification.

"Fuck me. That's Judge Barbara Portnoy."

I sat back in the passenger seat and stared at the computer screen for another five seconds or so, right up until Chipelo fumbled with the record button and turned off his body cam.

CHAPTER FIVE

DOMINIC

I arranged to meet Detective Ledsome for lunch on Friday. She had been surprised when I called her, and hadn't tried to hide it; but as we talked on the phone I heard something in her voice change, like she'd come across a chance to get something on me, an admission— or maybe catch me in a lie.

We sat across from each other at a picnic table beside a taco trailer on East Oltorf, close to my office but closer to a couple of housing projects, a shady gas station, and one of East Austin's under-performing middle schools. As a result, I paid in cash and made sure the badge in my wallet stayed hidden and the DA identification I wore around my neck was tucked away in my shirt pocket. But people came and went around us, paying no attention to anything except their bags of tacos and which salsa they should get. I knew the chick behind the counter, Esmie, and she gave me a look when she saw me sit opposite Ledsome, like I was trying to seduce the cop.

Already tried and failed, Esmie.

Ledsome unwrapped the foil from her taco and said, "I wasn't expecting to hear from you."

"Yeah, I thought maybe we should clear the air."

She took a bite, just chewing and watching as I poured green salsa on my chicken taco. Eventually she swallowed and said, "Go on."

"You've been asking questions about me. The kids in detention. I wondered why."

She smiled. "Juvenile delinquents. Who knew you couldn't trust them to keep their mouths shut?"

"Yeah, shocking."

"It's nothing official, Dom, you don't have to worry."

"Seems official, using your position and all to get access to the kids."

"There's no official investigation, that's what I mean."

"Just an unofficial one? Into what?"

She took another bite, then dabbed at her mouth with a paper napkin. "I've been receiving letters," she said.

"How very 1980s."

"They're not big on letting inmates use e-mail. Probably a good thing."

"You have a boyfriend in jail? How unusual for a cop."

"Not really a boyfriend," she said. "More of an informant."

"What does this have to do with me?"

"His name is Tristan Bell." As she spoke, her eyes never left my face, and I knew she was watching for a reaction.

So I laughed. "Are you serious?"

"Absolutely." Tristan Bell had been my roommate for less than a year, time he'd spent orchestrating the theft of cash from a trailer-park landlord. The heist had gone wrong, and the landlord and his bodyguard had wound up dead. So had Otto Bland, an accomplice of Tristan's. Even though I'd played a peripheral and unintentional role in the crime, very peripheral and unintentional, Tristan had tried to frame me for the whole thing. Ledsome, fortunately, had figured the framing part out, with a little help from yours truly.

"What does Tristan have to say?"

She shrugged and looked away. "You know, the usual. Mostly the usual. I mean, normally they claim they're innocent and have been screwed by the system, stuff like that. Tristan, he admits he was involved but disputes the role we attributed to him."

"Criminal mastermind," I proffered.

"Right."

"Let me guess, that was my role."

"That's the gist of it," Ledsome said. "And he sure does put a lot of detail in those letters."

I grunted and took a big bite. If she was looking to see signs of worry, she was in for a disappointment. Even if I were guilty of anything, one of the advantages of being a sociopath is that a guilty act didn't dress itself in a cloak of guilty emotions. I wasn't going to stammer or blush or shake with nerves. Not possible. Finally, I took a sip of my soda and said, "Any of his details check out?"

"That would be telling, wouldn't it?"

I sharpened my tone. "Yes, which is why I asked."

"He does raise some interesting questions. Like, where did all the money go? Did Otto really commit suicide? And who found out about Silva driving around East Austin with a van full of cash?"

"No clue."

"He says it was your buddy, Gus. He says Gus Cronstedt was Silva's immigration attorney, and he told you about the way Silva collected his rent in cash, drove around with it in his van." She was staring at me. "You know Gus, your good friend who coincidentally has disappeared."

"He left his wife," I said. "He's probably serving drinks at a bar in Costa Rica. That was his dream."

"Not as far as I can tell. His passport's not been used, and I can find no trace of his existence beginning about a week after the robbery."

"Do your bosses know you're conducting this investigation? Or should I call it a witch hunt? Does my boss, the DA know? Because I'm almost certain that if they found out, especially by reading about it in the newspapers, they would be less than happy."

She colored slightly. "I told you, there's no official investigation."

"And there shouldn't be an unofficial one, either." I sighed. "Look, Megan. He tried to frame me the first time around. Right? I mean you're the one who figured that out." She didn't say anything, just looked at me, so I went on. "Why would he stop trying to do that? I mean, he had one scheme, one trick up his sleeve, and he's still trying to play it. The guy now has all the time in the world to sit in prison and dream up gnarly little questions or vague theories just to get your juices flowing."

"Maybe," she conceded.

I let myself get a little hot. "No, not maybe. Definitely. I mean, Jesus, Megan. I'm a fucking prosecutor and he's a convicted murderer and pedophile. You're really believing the shit he's dishing up?"

"I don't know, Dominic; I'm just trying to do my job."

"You already did it!" I banged my hand on the table and ignored the looks from around us. "You saved my arse from that lunatic, and for some reason you're buying into his psycho little games, and at my expense."

"Calm down," she said. "I'm not buying into anything at this point, just looking into stuff."

"And that stuff happens to be me. Look, have you found something, *anything*, that substantiates what he's claiming?"

She thought for a moment. "No. Just those questions that I can't answer. About the money, and Otto. Gus's disappearance."

"Of course you can't answer them, only he can! And he knows damn well I can't—and he wants that to make me look guilty of something. But if I wasn't fucking involved, how the hell can I know?" I took a deep, calming breath. "It's like you're asking me to prove a negative, which I just can't do; it's not possible."

"Your friend Gus really took off from his wife like that?"

"Ask her." I took a bite of my taco. Ledsome was still holding hers, watching me.

"I did," she said.

"Great, so my best friend's wife now knows you're investigating me. Thanks for that."

"No, she doesn't. I didn't give her any details." Ledsome played with her straw. "And she couldn't give me any, either."

"That makes two of us."

"How about your little friend, Bobby? I got the impression he knows more than he's letting on."

"That kid." I shook my head. "He wants you, he wants everyone, to think he's smarter and tougher than he is. I'm trying to help him, in my own way, but he doesn't make it easier."

"Does your boss know you're dating his sister?"

Ah. "He tell you that?"

"Nope. Kinda figured you were all keeping it a secret."

"Yeah." I gave a rueful shake of my head. "That doesn't look good."

"No shit. You'd get fired."

"Maybe, but probably not. Like I said, I'm just trying to help him out. For his sister's sake as much as his."

"Good of you." I couldn't tell whether she was being sarcastic or not. "What's she like?"

"Different," I said, then: "Look, I can't stop you from doing whatever it is you're doing, but do me one favor. Give me the presumption of innocence, OK? If you have to go around asking questions . . . fine, I have nothing to hide from you. But for fuck's sake do it in a way that doesn't make me look guilty when you don't have any evidence, none at all, that I am."

"I can assure you, I'm very careful in what I do and say."

"If that were true, I don't think we'd be having this conversation."

"Sure we would. We're here because of those letters."

"Which you should be throwing away." I waved a hand. "Or recycling these days, I expect."

Her eyes narrowed. "I've always felt like there was something off about you, Dominic, something not quite right. And until I can put my finger on it, I'll keep reading Tristan Bell's letters."

"Fine, then read them all you like," I said. "I don't care what he has to say. But just have the decency not to drag my name through the mud unless and until you have a damn good reason to do so."

Before she could answer, I swung my legs out from under the table, stood up, and walked toward the barrel trash can, scrunching my taco wrappers into a ball and dunking them in. I felt her eyes on my back as I walked away, but she didn't say anything, which pleased me. I do like to have the last word.

O

I was surprised to find Brian at his desk when I got back. He wore jeans and a plaid shirt, and he looked worried.

"So much for my peace and quiet on Fridays," I said.

"Funny. I forgot to do a few things for my docket on Monday. Not used to preparing in advance."

"Yeah, I knew that about you. How was the ride-along?"

"Fine." His eyes darted away from me, and he looked uncomfortable. "You get your car fixed up?"

"I will. No real damage; insurance is covering it."

"Why did that old lady tell us you were being hostile?"

"I expect she was scared. Preemptive call, something like that, just in case I was mean."

McNulty smiled. "As if."

"Right? Picking on old ladies isn't my style. I prefer to pick on you. Speaking of which, your path to the judicial bench just got a little more crowded."

His eyes narrowed. "You didn't apply, did you?"

"I did." I gave him my most charming smile, the one where I crinkle my eyes a little, too. "But I only did that for the future, I have no intention or desire to get the job now. You know how it is; you have to show interest a couple of times before they take you seriously. Pay your dues and all that."

"Right, this is my third attempt."

"They may make an exception for one new candidate, though."

"Who is it?" he asked.

"Our very own Mo Barcinski."

"Shut up. Are you serious?"

"Dead serious." Mo had been our previous court chief, a quiet but very efficient and well-liked prosecutor.

"Fuck," McNulty said. "Portnoy and the other judges love her."

"I know; Portnoy tried to stop her getting transferred out of here. I'm guessing that means she'd welcome her to the bench with open arms."

"I have more experience than her in juvie. But, fuck," he said again.

"You want it that badly?"

"Yeah, I guess I do."

"Hey, it's not over until the fat lady sings. You'll do great in the interviews, and, like you said, she's not applied before and you have."

"Thing is," he said, in that irritating hangdog way, "I've been here five years. I don't know why but it seems like I'm never getting back downtown, to the trial courts. I suppose they might put me in Motor Fuel Tax Evasion, or some other bullshit division, but I don't want that. This place is close to my apartment, close to the gym . . ." He shrugged.

"You go to the gym?"

"Fuck off, Dom, you know what I mean."

"That you want that judge job." I swung my feet onto the desk.

"Trust me, moping around and assuming you've lost out isn't going to help. You have to go to those interviews and act like you're already a judge. You know the law, now you need to show them you'd be good in that role, too."

"Yeah, I guess."

I picked up an offense report, a seventy-pager, and started reading, highlighter in hand, and tuned Brian out. But after a few minutes he spoke up. "Hey, I need to get some evidence for this one case."

Something we learn to do on the first day. "And?"

"Well, I know we can download the in-car video from the dash cam, but I can't remember if we can do the same thing for the new body cameras."

"Yes." I refrained from rolling my eyes. Brian was one of those people you had to explain things to three times, and show him four times, before he got it. "Same Versadex portal as for in-car video, but different drop-down menu. Otherwise, all the same."

"Right," he said, but didn't sound sure.

"Do I need to show you again?"

"No, I just . . . it's in the offense report, the photo . . . that's what I needed. I'm good, thanks."

Hardly good, I thought, but as long as he left me alone for the rest of the afternoon, I'd have nothing more to say.

MEGAN

Megan Ledsome checked her phone as it rang, and realized it was almost nine in the evening.

"Hey, Greg," she said. "I just saw what time it is. Sorry."

"No problem, babe, I was just checking on you." People had told her not to date, let alone marry, another cop—"inevitable disaster," they'd said. But not with Greg. For one thing, he understood when she had to work late, when she got deep into a case and forgot to check the time, or eat.

"Thanks," she said. "We have any of that pizza left?"

"We do. I'll heat you a couple of slices. Salad too?"

"And a large glass of wine."

"Done. You leaving now?"

Ledsome stood and looked down at her mess of a desk. "Hell yes. I'm not solving anything tonight."

"OK. We can talk about it when you get home, if you think it'd help."

"Sure, it might. See you in a few."

She disconnected and walked through the quiet of the police station, seeing only a handful of other cops and a couple of cleaners. She waved at the two guys manning the front desk, and pushed the door open. The night was clear and bright, a full moon beaming down over the city, and she breathed in the fresh air as she crossed Eighth Street to get to the garage. She had an idea, somewhere she wanted to check before heading home. Greg wouldn't mind, and if she just cruised past the place her pizza would still be warm.

Tomorrow she'd take another run at a couple of the kids who had acted weird when she talked to them. That Bobby kid included. Something about him wasn't right, sitting across the table from each other, and they both knew it. Something in his eyes, which managed to seem both dead and amused at the same time. Many times in her career she'd sat across from people who claimed, or suggested, that they knew more than they did. Bobby managed to do it without saying a word. What this kid could know about Dominic she had no clue, but a sparkle in his eyes was enough to bring her back to him, to try to coax something out of him.

She took Eighth Street to Congress Avenue, then turned left. Traffic was light; it was too early for the weekend revelers to be out yet, and she made quick progress on her way south over the Congress Avenue Bridge and up to Oltorf Avenue, where she turned left and drove over the always-busy I-35. As every Austin cop knew, or quickly learned, I-35 was where the city changed.

Whether you lived north or south, that long band of asphalt was a border. To the west of it lay downtown, and further west the safe and expensive communities of Tarrytown and Westlake. To the east lived Austin's working class and poor, communities like Dove Springs, a place that Ledsome knew had seen neither doves nor springs in forever. That side of the city families of six, seven, or eight piled into two- and three-bedroom houses, such that the kids' toys and bikes lived mostly in the front yards, scattered around the old cars that blocked driveways while they waited to be fixed.

Detective Ledsome took Oltorf toward Wickersham Lane, slowing as a light changed from green to red. The cars around her all stopped, no one trying to beat the light. In her experience, the light-running was done mostly by the scofflaws on the west side of town, the people in their Audis and Land Rovers whose time was too precious to be spent dawdling at an intersection. There was another reason, too, she knew. Out here, a higher proportion of folks on the road either had outstanding warrants or weren't in the country legally, both good reasons to observe and abide by traffic laws, all of them.

She checked her phone, pleased that there was nothing new from work, and put it away. She looked up to check the light, still red, and worried that Greg might actually be annoyed at her detour. She should've told him. She reached for her phone again to text him but stopped when she saw movement in her rearview mirror.

Someone crossing the street? But the crosswalk was in front of her.

She turned to look out of the window behind her, surprised to see a figure walking between her car and the one on her left. She couldn't see his face, just his body, a slender figure in what she guessed was a hoodie.

She pressed the button to wind her window down, planning to give this idiot a lecture about not getting run over, and she made sure her police ID badge was visible on her chest.

"Hey, buddy," she said, and the figure stopped beside her. "If you're crossing the road, use the crosswalk. If you're not, get out of the street. My colleagues don't appreciate having to scrape people like you off the—"

She saw the gun and fell silent, her eyes widening as it pointed at her face through the open window. Her mind spun like tires in the snow, and she couldn't move, couldn't speak. Finally she found words, her voice cracking as she said, "Put that away. I'm a cop."

"I know," the voice said gently, unconcerned.

Then the figure stooped down, and Ledsome was able to drag her eyes away from the gun. She'd been right, he was wearing a hoodie, and it framed his face perfectly. A face she recognized immediately, particularly those eyes, cold and knowing eyes that managed to look amused at her terror.

"No one tells us what to do," he said, and before she could reply, Detective Megan Ledsome saw the trigger give way, felt for just a split second her ears exploding and a searing pain that ripped through her chest before feeling, all of a sudden, nothing at all.

She slumped to her right just as the light changed from red to green, a change that made no difference to anything because the other six cars at the intersection had already gone, peeling away left and right the moment the first shot rang out. Drivers in this part of town didn't linger to take photos or video, to give witness statements or try to help. No, East Austin was where you looked out for yourself and your family; and if someone else had a beef that required a person get shot, you looked the other way or, if you could, you drove the other way.

The figure in the hoodie finished crossing the road, not looking behind him, the gun going back into his waistband, the barrel warm against his skin. *Should I pick up the shell casings?* he wondered for a moment, then he smiled to himself. *Fuck it, the cops can have them. I already got away with it.*

As he turned down a quiet lane, he pushed his shoulders back and walked with the confidence of someone who carries a gun and knows he's not afraid to use it. The sound of sirens drifted over him, but by the time the cops realized they were dealing with murder, he was a mile away. And by the time someone spotted a badge through the blood and called for the police helicopter, he was just another guy in a hoodie waiting at a bus stop and minding his own business, playing with his phone and wondering where he might grab a bite to eat.

CHAPTER SIX

DOMINIC

On Saturday morning, I rolled out of bed at eight, thinking about hitting the gym. I was playing at the Continental Club that night but otherwise had nothing much to do and felt an energy in my body that I didn't like, a pull toward some undefined mischief. An hour at the gym would calm me down, right my mood, and leave me the rest of the day to practice or maybe write more music.

And then I fired up my computer and started looking at the news.

The lead story on the *Austin Statesman*, and on every TV station, was the shooting of a cop in cold blood. As I took in the details, my jaw clenched. Apparently Detective Megan Ledsome had pulled up to a stoplight on East Oltorf. According to the newspaper report, which cited an unnamed eyewitness, a car containing two or three juveniles had pulled up next to her, and one of them had gotten out and walked up to the stationary Ledsome, shooting her numerous times. The reports all noted that police gathered nine empty casings from the scene, and that she'd been hit five times. Dead before the light changed color. I skimmed each article and felt a tinge of relief that no suspects were in custody. But only a tinge.

I picked up my cell phone and dialed a small house on the other side of town.

"Hey, it's me," I said when she picked up. "Is Bobby there?"

"No, he went out last night and didn't come home."

"Fuck. You let him go out?"

She sighed, sounded tired. "How exactly am I supposed to stop him?"

"Does he have a phone with him?"

"Why do you need him?"

"A surprise. Can you text me his cell number?"

"Sure."

A thought struck me. "Does his phone have that tracking device on it? Find iPhone or whatever?"

"Dom. We can't afford iPhones, it's a crappy one from like the 1990s."

"Yeah, sorry. If you hear from him, though, have him call me straightaway, will you? It's important."

I'd tried to keep my tone light, but she caught something. "What's wrong? Is he in trouble?"

Understatement of the year, I thought. "Not that I can prove," I said jokingly. "I gotta run; I'll check in with you. Oh, wait. Is his monitor there?"

"I don't know. I mean, I assume he's wearing it."

"If he is, and his PO asks why he went out, tell him you were with him."

"I know that, Dom, I was in the courtroom. Anyway, can't you just track him?"

"We don't have access to that, no. Only his PO does. See if it's in his room, a lot of kids wriggle out of them if they're not fitted right."

I waited, listening to the sounds of her moving through the house and into his room. She was quiet for a moment, then said, "I don't see it anywhere; he must be wearing it. That's good, right? He can get in trouble for taking it off."

"Yeah," I said. "He sure can." *But he can get in a damn sight more trouble if he wears it to the scene of a murder.* I rang off and dropped my phone onto the table.

"That fucking kid," I said to the wall. "What the hell do we do now?"

My phone buzzed, and Bobby's name and number appeared in a text. I started to dial it, then realized that would be a mistake. If he had done this, and if he was found with his phone on him, then the police would be talking to every name on his call list. If they did that, saw my number, and then found out about Ledsome's unofficial investigation, I'd be a much larger dot on the radar than I wanted to be. Not to mention my boss connecting me with a kid I was prosecuting, although at this point that seemed like a minor concern. My new policy of talking to the kids in detention had broken that formerly impenetrable barrier between prosecutors and kids, but even so I had no real desire to test how far that rule might bend.

I needed to talk to Bobby, though, so I drove from my apartment on South Congress to a gas station in East Austin where I paid cash for a prepaid phone. Useful things, prepaids. I sat in my car and dialed Bobby's number, but it went straight to voicemail.

I was just about to drive home when my cell phone rang. It was a 974 prefix, the Austin Police Department. Figured I better answer.

"This is Dominic."

"Dominic, hello. My name's Sergeant Jeremy Brannon from the Austin Police Homicide Division, I hope you don't mind, but I got your cell number from your division manager."

"That's fine, how can I help?"

"I'm sure you heard about my colleague Megan Ledsome's shooting."

"Yes, I did. I'm shocked—I'm sure you all are as well."

"Yeah, thanks. So, the thing is, we're moving on it as fast as we can. We have a few leads but need to tie things off where we can. Oh, I forgot, you OK with me recording this conversation?"

"Absolutely, no problem at all."

"Great. So like I said, it's easier for us to focus on the real leads if we can get rid of the ones we're pretty sure are duds."

"Of course, how can I help?"

"You had lunch with Megan on Friday. Yesterday."

"That's right." My mind started spinning. Did they already know about her unofficial investigation? If not, should I tell them? If they did know and I didn't say anything . . .

"You guys are friends?"

"No, I wouldn't go that far. We got to know each other a little during a trial I had. And then with that robbery-murder business. . . . She basically saved my life, so I was grateful."

"And yet she paid for her own lunch yesterday."

You've done your homework. "Yeah." I laughed. "I offered but she insisted, didn't think it proper."

"Was there a reason for the meeting?" Brannon asked.

"Kind of, yes. She wanted to let me know that she'd been receiving letters from the guy convicted in that case—"

"Tristan Bell."

Again, impressed. "That's right."

"Why was she receiving letters from him?"

"You'd have to ask him," I said. "Do you know about that case?"

"Of course, yes."

"Then you'll know he tried to frame me back then. From what Megan said, he's still trying to."

"He still says you're involved?"

"Apparently. And not just involved, but the mastermind."

"Huh."

I hated doing this over the phone. After a life spent reading people's faces, I felt like I was being handicapped here. This Brannon guy gave nothing away in his tone, which stayed pleasant but to the point. "Did you feel like she was reinvestigating the case? Reinvestigating you?"

"No, not at all. I mean, I don't know if she actually was or not, but I can't see why. And the way she was talking, it was just letting me know that Bell was still at it, still trying to put it all on me."

"Did you arrange to see her again?"

"No."

"And, forgive me for asking, but was there anything romantic between the two of you?"

"No, not at all." *Not for the want of me trying, though.*

"Had to ask."

"No problem, I know how it is."

"One other thing," he said. "We understand she was visiting some juveniles while they were in detention. Any idea why?"

"None whatsoever."

"Did you know that she was?"

I paused, then lied. "I didn't, no. She wasn't working on any juvenile cases?"

"Haven't had a juvenile commit murder in Austin for over a year."

"Thankful for small mercies, eh?"

His turn to pause, and I wondered if I'd done what I sometimes do when I don't pick up on the emotional component of a situation. I can appear callous or flippant, both of which I am but neither of which I want to sound like.

"Yeah, I guess that's about right," he said. "Well, if I can think of any other questions, I'll be in touch."

"Please. Anything I can do to help, anything at all."

"We appreciate it," he said, and hung up.

I ran the conversation back in my mind, wondering if I'd slipped up, said anything to cause him to be suspicious. Bad enough if Bobby had done this, but if Ledsome's murder caused APD to look into the heist and its associated murders all over again . . . Well, to put it mildly, my life could be uncomfortable for a while.

All of which paled into nothingness when I thought about Bobby, because they'd almost certainly catch him. He was a smart kid, but not as smart as he thought, and not nearly as smart as the combined resources of Austin's Homicide Division and whatever other agencies they brought in to help.

And this left me with one question: *if* he's guilty, and they get him, what will he say?

O

On the drive home, I started thinking about the news reports. They'd mentioned *two or three* juveniles in the car. Bobby had a few friends, but they were such a rotating bunch of delinquents that at any one time half his group was locked up. I had no way of knowing whether one of that lot who was out in the free would be dumb enough to go along with a plan to kill a cop.

Maybe under the influence of drugs . . .? But other than the occasional joint, Bobby didn't do drugs. Most of his friends dabbled, but he was like me in that life was exciting enough without resorting to illegal substances. As far as I knew, anyway.

I needed to see the official police report, see if it contained any more information from the crime scene, witness statements, anything I could use to find Bobby before the cops did.

And when I found him, my plan was simple: turn him in.

He'd have a lawyer by his side, for sure, one whom I'd pick and one who would advise him to keep his mouth shut at all times. The moment you're captured and the police want to talk to you, that is the most dangerous time for any suspect, adult or juvenile. As soon as you ask for a lawyer, they'll stop, but up until then you're fair game; and I knew full well that in a murder investigation, and one involving a cop no less, they'd use every trick in the book to get a story from Bobby before he lawyered up.

I pulled up the office calendar on my phone to see who was staffing the DA's office. One prosecutor was always on standby in the main office, and one from juvenile was always available, too. While they didn't *have* to hang around the office, I knew that when Brian was on call he often did. Loser.

Sure enough, Brian was at his desk when I called.

"Hey, Dom. You calling to invite me to lunch?"

"Have I ever?"

"True. Maybe when I'm a judge, eh?"

"I don't fraternize with men in robes." I softened my tone, reminding myself that I was calling because I needed his help. "But you never know, we'll see."

"That's good enough for me. What do you need?"

"You heard about that detective who got shot?"

"Yeah, I was just reading about it. Wasn't she a friend of yours?"

"She was, which is why I'm calling. I don't want to bug the detectives working the case, but I want to know more about it."

"Oh, you want to see the offense report?"

"Sure, if you don't mind," I said. "I know it's far from complete, but it may have a few witness statements, that kind of thing."

"Gonna solve it yourself?"

"No," I laughed along. "Just with her being my friend, you know . . ."

"I'll log onto Versadex and download it. Want me to e-mail it to you?"

Versadex was the system APD used for logging all of their reports and videos. Prosecutors had been given access to the reports for some time, but only recently had we been able to download in-car and other videos, too.

"Yes, please, save me a trip down there."

"You live, like, half a mile away."

"I'm at my girlfriend's this weekend."

"What's she like?"

"She's not like anything, or anyone." I smiled. "She's sexy and subversive, and likes to fuck with authority."

"When do I meet her?" he asked. Like he was my fucking dad.

"When it becomes serious. Fair?"

"Sure. All right, dude, logging in now. Putting in her name . . ." I could hear his heavy fingers on the keyboard. "Oh, shit. It's locked."

"Locked?"

"Yeah, says it's an ongoing investigation and it's locked. Gives a Sergeant Jeremy Brannon's name, if you want more information."

"I have his contact info, but don't want to bug him. Oh well, thanks for trying, Brian, much obliged."

"Sure. See ya Monday."

I'd used my burner and rang off without saying good-bye.

Dead end.

Yet Bobby had to be somewhere, and I needed to find him before the cops even started looking. The only thing I could think to do was ask the one person who knew him best. But that meant coming clean with her about what he'd done, and even though she was the coolest, most collected empath I knew, Bobby was her weakness, and I had no idea how she'd react.

One way to find out.

"Hey, it's me," I said. "Any word from Bobby?"

"No. What's going on, Dominic?"

"That cop that got shot. You see that?"

"Yes. She's the one who investigated the robbery."

"She went to see Bobby in detention recently. Was asking questions about his and my involvement in that."

"Wait, seriously? Why didn't you tell me?"

"I'm telling you now. I just talked to her yesterday."

"And?"

"And the other night when you went out for his birthday pizza, Bobby was saying some nasty stuff about what he could do to her."

A pause. "You better be kidding."

"I'm not. I was very, very clear with him that doing anything, even keying her bloody car, would be a disastrous idea. I explained it to him, that they'd come after a cop killer with everything under the sun. I thought he'd understood."

"That's ridiculous," she said. Her voice was matter-of-fact, and I was relieved she was being so calm. "There's no way he'd do something like that."

"I know, I agree. I'm just telling you what's going on, why for my peace of mind I want to talk to him."

"You think he's capable of doing that, don't you?"

"We both know that, in theory, he's more than capable of it."

"He wouldn't do that," she insisted.

"And yet someone did."

"He has no reason to kill her. He wouldn't do that. He may be impulsive, but he knows better."

"He's a teenage psychopath."

"I know what he is, Dominic."

"Yeah, well, I was one too, which means I can see this through his eyes, and you need to, as well. He's seeing a cop who is investigating a double homicide and who basically tells him she thinks he's involved. He's seeing a quick, easy, and permanent way out of that. He's impulsive, thinks he's smarter than everyone around him." I paused, not thrilled about admitting the last factor, the one she would appreciate the least. "And he had a grown-up telling him he shouldn't do it, couldn't get away with it. We're not good with authority, neither of us, and it's possible that my little talk had the opposite of its intended effect."

She didn't speak for a moment. When she did, her voice was soft, almost resigned. "This is what I was always afraid of. Not the smoking weed or shoplifting, but something big. Something like this, that he'd do it before realizing more about himself, understanding himself."

"Look, it's possible I'm wrong. I hope for all our sakes that I am. But in the meantime we need to find him."

"Do the police know? Are they looking for him?"

"I don't think so. I doubt it, not yet, but they will."

"What's the best thing for him to do?"

I thought I heard something in her voice, wondered for a second if she was holding out on me.

"Do you know where he is?" I asked.

"No, I don't. But if he comes home I want to know what to do."

"Have him call me and sit tight until I get there. Whether he did this or not, he'll need a lawyer next to him any time he talks to the cops."

"OK."

"In the meantime, do you have any idea where he might be? Or . . . where he might have gotten his hands on a gun?"

"His friends . . . who knows? I'm sure he could if he really wanted to. We both know that."

We did. Bobby wasn't in any of the East Austin gangs, but he floated around them, circling here and landing there, more like a hornet than a butterfly, courted for his special skills, for his lack of fear and his intelligence. As I well knew, the boy could steal a car in five seconds flat and drive it away like an adult. Which is to say, with one eye out for the cops, observing traffic laws that his idiot brethren didn't even know existed.

Which made me think that he could also stay hidden, if need be. At the very least, get rid of a gun that might incriminate him.

"It's OK," I said. "I have an idea."

"What?"

"You said his monitor isn't there?"

"Right. I assumed he was wearing it, but if he did this . . . Would he keep it on?"

"It wouldn't be so smart," I said. "But he wouldn't be the first kid to track himself to a crime scene. I can't think he'd be that dumb, but I don't know what else to do."

"You mean, locate him using the monitor?"

"Yes. Locate the monitor at the very least."

"But that'll attract attention from his PO. Won't he have to alert someone?"

"Not the way I'll do it. The PO is a friend of mine; we can do it unofficially."

"If you say so." For the first time, she sounded unsure. Like she trusted us to figure it out, just the two of us, and didn't want to bring anyone else in. I wasn't wild about the idea myself, but I didn't know where else to turn.

I rang off and dialed Brian McNulty again.

"Hey, old chap," I said. "So how about that lunch after all?"

CHAPTER SEVEN

I picked McNulty up from the front of the Juvenile Justice Center, called Gardner Betts but known as "GB" or "the Betts." He stood on the curb, grinning and waving like a little boy waiting for his mum to pick him up after school.

"Hey man, I'm starving," he said. "Where to?"

"How about Curra's? I could use some Mexican."

He frowned. "I don't know, Dom, you know what happened last time I ate there."

"That was a one-off," I assured him. "Any restaurant can serve up one bad meal. I've eaten there a dozen times since and been fine."

"If you say so." He didn't sound convinced.

"My treat," I said. "That way if you spend the next week on the toilet you won't have wasted a dime."

"Sure, OK."

The place was barely a mile away and actually served good Mexican food from the Michoacán state of Mexico. The only thing better than their tacos carnitas plate was the "café Oaxaca," smoky and strong, with just a hint of vanilla, it was the best cup of coffee in Austin.

We were shown to a booth by the window, and McNulty tucked into the chips and salsa.

"We're friends enough that I can double-dip, right?" he asked.

"No."

"Sure we are." He double-dipped, still crunching the first half of a large chip, and I resisted, only just, the temptation to put my fork through his eyeball. "So how come the change of mind?"

"I realized I had to come to the office anyway, a little work to do."

"Oh, that sucks."

"From the man who voluntarily comes in on Saturdays."

"Yeah, well, if I want that judge job, I gotta look eager."

"Oh, please, juvenile judges are the laziest people on the planet."

"You think?" He looked surprised.

"Yeah, the job'll suit you perfectly."

He laughed and wagged a finger. "Oh, very funny. You'll be in so much trouble when I get that robe."

"If you get it."

His expression fell. "Oh, yeah. Mo's application."

"Did you call her?" I asked. "You know, to see if she really wants the job. Maybe if she realizes how much it means to you, she'll back off."

"I did. She was being all coy, acting like she wasn't interested, didn't know anything about it."

"That's a bad sign," I said.

"Yeah, I know. But even though she's senior to me, like at the DA's office, I have more years practicing juvenile law." He shrugged. "Plus, Judge Portnoy likes me, and I have a few cards up my sleeve."

That right there was one of the more annoying things he did. Acting like he knew more than he did, or had some secret that he would reveal only if he needed to. I'd heard him do it in plea negotiations with defense lawyers, pretend some special piece of evidence was about to magically appear and make his case a slam dunk. I picked up my fork and ran a thumb across the pointy tines, imagining but not doing what I wanted to do.

"I'll get us some of that good coffee," I said, sliding out of the booth. Normally one of the waitresses brought it, but I'd been there so often that they didn't mind me helping myself, and I needed a few moments away from the chip-chomping moron opposite me.

I put his cup in front of him and dropped a few little pots of creamer on the table.

"Couldn't remember how you take it."

"Sweet and creamy, like I take my women," he said with a wink.

"Women, plural?"

"Well, not right now. Connie would kill me." He laughed. "Although I could always ask; she's pretty wild."

"Lucky you."

The waitress came over and hugged me, nodding enthusiastically at Brian. "How you guys doing? Same as usual, Dom?"

"Yes, please."

"I'll have that, too," Brian said.

When the waitress had left, I asked him, "Do you even know what you just ordered?"

"Nope," he said cheerfully. "But I trust your judgment. And there's basically nothing on this planet I don't eat."

"Why doesn't that surprise me?"

"I know, right? That's why I work out a lot; I love food too much."

He did. He seemed to be eating nonstop at the office, and when our lunch plates arrived he spent an entire minute wafting his pudgy nose over the plate, identifying the various aromas, like a wine sommelier performing to an impressed audience. Except, of course, I wasn't impressed, just exceptionally annoyed.

BRIAN

There's one thing I'll say about Dominic: he knows the good places to eat. I was reluctant at first because the last time I was here, with him and a couple of others from work, I ate something that severely disagreed with me. For, like, three days.

But these tacos carnitas were amazing, the meat slow-roasted and soaked in Coca-Cola, wrapped tightly in fresh tortillas, and topped with green salsa made on-site. I finished before Dom had eaten his first, but that gave me time to enjoy the coffee.

He's an odd one, that Dominic. Like, he acts so grumpy and mean sometimes, but he's actually quite kind. Thoughtful. He really likes this place, always talks it up and wants me to enjoy it, too. That's why I put up with his bullshit, because it's all for show. I'm betting it's that English thing, stiff upper lip and all that. Can't actually show any emotion, the Queen wouldn't approve.

I often asked him about growing up there; I'm kind of fascinated with things English, especially royalty. And from what he's told me, that was his life. Boarding schools, pheasant shooting, tea and scones. He can be a little tight-lipped if I act overly interested, but he's got some good stories.

One thing I've noticed, though, is that he doesn't say much about his parents. About all I know is that they died in a freak accident about a year ago. His dad stepped on a power line that came down in a storm, and his mom didn't realize, went to help him up, and *zap*. Both dead. Maybe that's why he doesn't talk about them at all—still too upset. Plus, I get the impression he didn't get a lot of hugs as a kid, not that kind of family. Kinda sad.

Back at the office, we sat at our desks and logged into our work computers, quiet for a moment. He doesn't like too much talking, and sometimes I can't help myself, so I tried to give him a few moments of peace and quiet.

"Dammit," Dominic said.

"What's up?"

"I can't get into Versadex. Is yours working?"

"Let me check." As useful as it was to have direct access to APD's reports and videos, the system glitches quite a lot. I clicked on the icon, entered my username and password and waited. "Yep, I'm good. What do you need?"

"A 911 call, I think," Dom said. "But let me finish reading this report, make sure I need it."

Two minutes later, it struck. I felt my stomach rumbling, and in that bad way, where you know you're in deep trouble.

"Fuck, Dom, I told you."

"What?"

"That food. That place. It doesn't agree with me."

"Are you serious? Again?"

"Yes. I don't get it—I ate the same thing as you!"

"You sure you don't have allergies? My friend's mum has a dairy allergy, sends her screaming to the bathroom when she so much looks at cheese."

"No, dude, I don't have any food allergies, I think I'd know." I didn't mean to sound irritated, but I was. Not so much with him; it wasn't his fault that place didn't agree with me. I was annoyed at myself for letting him talk me into going. I stood, then doubled over with a cramp in my guts. "Oh, fuck. I'll be back in a while."

I almost ran to the bathrooms. Thankfully it was Saturday so the place was empty, because I actually thought I was going to have an accident on the way. *Must be the pork*, I thought. *Every time I've gotten sick, it's been from pork. Could I actually be allergic to it?*

I stayed in the stall through several rounds, and when I stepped out and looked in the mirror, I was sweating. But I felt better, a little, and made my way back to the office. Dominic had left already, but he'd pulled up a Word document on my computer and left a nice note.

I feel bad about making you eat at Curra's, I hope you're feeling better. I had to run, one of those pseudo-girlfriend emergencies. See ya Monday. D.

I couldn't help but chuckle. Connie was an angel but sometimes blew things out of proportion, so I knew what he was talking about. I was curious, too, because he never talked about his girlfriend, and I'd not met her. What kind of woman gets a man like Dominic? A hot one, I'd bet. Smart, too, because he didn't suffer fools.

My office phone rang and it was Dominic; he apologized again, like it was his fault.

"A suggestion that might help," he said.

"God, Dom, anything, please."

"We do this in England, at least my family does. On your way home, stop by that fancy gas station on Lamar. Buy a six-pack of Guinness."

"Dude, I hate that stuff."

"I know, I know. But it'll help. Drink one as soon as you get home, then another after each toilet visit."

"That's gross. And no way Connie would let me."

"Of course she won't. Get a slushy cup from the gas station and use that."

I waited to see if he was kidding, but even Dom wouldn't screw with me in my state. "OK, I guess it can't hurt."

"Something about the iron helps. Try it."

O

DOMINIC

While Brian was indisposed, I sent just one e-mail, to Bobby's PO:

> *Hey, can I get a huge favor? I need to know where one of your kids has been, and where he is now. Trying to figure out if we need to modify his probation terms, my chief has told me to keep an eye on him. I put some specific dates and times below. His Juvie number is 89773. Best not to email me back, I'll be out of the office for a few days, so just call me with the info or, if I don't answer, leave me a voicemail on my cell, the number is below. Thanks!*

I headed back to my apartment to wait for the call back. It came less than an hour later, and I let it go to voicemail.

"Hey dude, sorry, I don't think I can do that. My boss sent out a memo two weeks ago about sharing GPS records with you guys. I thought y'all got it, too. Anyway, you have to get a subpoena to see them. Sorry!"

I closed the phone and sat back in my armchair to think.

CHAPTER EIGHT

BRIAN

I slept horribly on Sunday night, my stomach still messing with me, but even so on Monday morning I tried to get up and go to work. I felt lightheaded and had to steady myself against the wall when I stood up. Connie told me to stay home, and since I didn't have any cases set, I figured no harm, no foul. She had to go to work but said she'd come by at lunchtime to check on me, wouldn't take no for an answer on that. Angel, like I said. So when the doorbell rang at noon, I wasn't surprised; I assumed she'd forgotten her key. I was a little more surprised when I opened the door.

"Dominic. What are you doing here?"

We'd never been close, and him taking me to lunch and checking on me was weird, and I kinda thought maybe he was trying to suck up a little for when I get the judge job. Which I actually didn't mind, because I'm a realist and know how the world works. In any case, there's something about being on his good side that I like. I'm flawed enough to recognize my own weakness in that regard.

"Nice pj's, man," he joked. "You don't dress for your guests? The neighbors will talk."

"Oh, dude, sorry, I didn't—"

"I'm kidding, come on, Brian, get with it."

"Oh, sorry." That's how out of it I was, I didn't get his jokes. "You wanna come in?"

"No, it's okay, I was just out running errands. Did you try the Guinness trick?"

"Ugh. I *tried* to try it, but Connie busted me on the way in the door. Said it was ridiculous."

"And because she's a nurse, she knows best?"

"Basically."

"And yet here you are, still sick."

"Right? I know."

"Well, you're in luck." He held up a plastic bag. "Your medicine."

"Seriously, you brought me some?"

"Well, like I told you, I feel bad about taking you there." He opened the bag and I reached in and took out a six-pack. "Here you go."

"Thanks, man. I'm willing to try anything at this point."

He frowned. "Although, Connie's right in that we don't want you overdoing it. Tear off half of those cans and put them in the bag." He held it open while I did so. "Three should be plenty, anyway."

"And easier to stash three than six, out of sight of my conventional nurse," I said, with a wink. "Thanks again, Dom."

"Sure, no problem. One other thing—didn't you tell me a couple months ago that you play poker?"

"Yeah, sure do. Haven't played in a while, though."

"Cool," he said. "So this may be too rich for your blood, but once a year me and some mates get together and go all out for an evening."

"Oh yeah?"

"Helluva buy in, and, like I said, it might be too much for you, but one of our regulars dropped out, and I said I knew someone who might fill in."

"Me?" I was surprised he was asking, but flattered, too. Dom the musician, the prosecutor, the guy who'd helped solve a double homicide and almost gotten himself killed doing it. He was real picky about his friends, and I'd never seen myself as one. But with lunch the other day, the Guinness today, and now this . . . it had to be the judge thing.

"Sure, why not you?" he said.

"Yeah, OK. I'm in. Where and when?"

"Don't you want to know the buy in?"

"Oh yeah. How much?"

"Two grand. Cash. No checks or IOUs. Five people, so you can walk away with a helluva stash of cash, or lose big. That's the main thing, Brian, you have to be prepared to lose the entire two Gs and not be a baby about it."

I couldn't tell if that was a jab at me, whether he thought I was a baby. It was a lot of money, but I didn't want him to know I thought so. I tried to sound flippant. "I probably have that much lying around my apartment. It's no problem at all."

"OK." He paused, then said, "So we're clear, gambling this kind of money is illegal."

I didn't know that and my mouth suddenly went dry. "It is? You sure?"

"Yes," he said. "That's why we play for fun, not money. The two grand is for . . . other things. You know, the pleasure of my company."

"Right, of course. I figured." Relief washed over me, and I grinned. "Hey, you sure that's not illegal too?"

"Good one. Anyway, because of the whole legality shit, I'll send you a text with the details—day, time, place. Not from my phone, though."

"Roughly when?" I asked. Connie would need advance notice; she was an angel as a nurse but could be a little clingy.

"This weekend, maybe early next week. Don't flake on us, man."

"I won't, don't worry." Even if Connie didn't like it, this was a cool thing for me. Poker with Dominic and friends. I just needed to stay sober, otherwise I'd not only lose all my money but end up looking like an idiot. I decided that my main priority at that poker game would be getting invited back to a second one, and if that meant a few loose bets, so be it. It would be an investment. I'd look at it like that and hope Dominic didn't figure out that I was kinda playing him.

O

DOMINIC

I still needed to find Bobby.

That afternoon, I parked in the almost-empty parking lot outside the Dove Springs Rec Center on Ainez Drive in East Austin. A few people lingered outside, but their eyes were more into my car than me. I'd tried to dress down, changing from my suit to jeans and a raggedy sweatshirt, but I wasn't about to have my trousers hang below my arse like these people.

My observations were interrupted when my phone rang. The name Bernadette Graves Phillips appeared on the screen. She was the owner and manager of the hottest music venue in Austin, Club Steamboat, a place that had graced Austin for twenty-two years, closed in 1999, and reappeared with much fanfare six months ago.

By reopening the club Bernadette had become an Austin legend. She was fifty-something, dressed exuberantly, had an encyclopedic knowledge of local music, and knew pretty much everyone in the business. I knew her because she'd been a paralegal for the DA's office for thirty years before winning several million in the state lottery and quitting on the spot to live her dream—reviving an old institution and inviting her favorite musicians to play every night of the week.

"Dominic, can you play next Monday night?"

"Me and who else?"

"Just you. Main feature."

"I think that's for movies."

She cackled with laughter. "Maybe. Yes or no?"

"No."

"Because of the tips?"

"No one goes to clubs on Mondays so, yeah, the tips and playing to empty chairs. Not my idea of a wild night."

"This place is full every night. Mostly."

"For now. Things will slide, Bernie, they always do, and in six months I'll find myself in the Monday night slot playing to a couple of regular drunks and the cleaning lady with her mop in the corner. I have a glamorous reputation to uphold."

"Yeah, well. How about whatever you make in tips, I match."

I knew why she wanted me there. We were friends, yes, but even a year after the Tristan Bell heist I was still kind of a celebrity, the prosecutor-musician with the cool accent who'd narrowly, but bravely, avoided being framed for murder. Cachet right there.

"Two times zero still comes to zero," I said. "But if you're up for risking some cash, let's have a wee wager."

"Like what?"

"Average crowd for a Monday night is small, agreed?"

"Relatively, I guess so."

"How about I fill the place for you. Earn myself two hundred in tips. You'll double that."

"Wait," she said. "You'll make yourself two hundred and I pay you four hundred on top?"

"Think of the beer sales. All that Chardonnay you'll sell."

"And how do you propose to pack the place on a Monday night?" she asked.

"That's my problem. You game?"

She was quiet for a moment. I don't know why; it's not like money mattered to her anyway. "Hell, yes, of course I'm in. I'll advertise you for nine p.m."

"Make it eight. I'm not as young as I used to be."

We rang off, and I smiled. I do like a nice wager now and again.

I wandered into the Dove Springs Rec Center, but there were no kids in there, not of Bobby's age. I was pretty sure I'd recognize his two best buddies, Anton and Ledarius. Well, certain in Anton's case because I'd refreshed my recollection with his mug shot. Ledarius didn't have one of those, but he was pretty distinctive-looking, and I'd seen him two or three times in passing.

Neither boy was inside, as I discovered when I wandered slowly through the place. Nicer than I'd imagined, with furniture in decent shape and more facilities than just a broken pool table and gum on the windowsills. My expectations hadn't been high.

I stood by a window, waiting, watching people come and go, watching the small groups outside. I was there less than two minutes when I saw Anton approach the entrance. He wore either jeans that were way too short, or denim shorts that were way too long. He walked with a swagger, like he owned the place, but once inside he paused and looked a little lost. I went up to him.

"Anton. Can I talk to you?"

He looked at me for a moment, then said, "I know you. You're the prosecutor on my case." His eyes narrowed. "You ain't supposed to talk to me."

"About your case, true. But I'm not here about that."

"What, then?"

"Your brother-in-arms, Bobby."

"Bobby who?"

"Right, and when I give you his last name you'll be all, *No idea who that is, mister.* Cut the crap. I may not be here on your case, but do you really think I'm going to forget our conversation here today, whichever way it goes?"

"Fuck you, you can't do that."

"Chill, kid. I'm already doing it."

"I'll tell my attorney and he'll tell the judge."

"Who won't believe a fucking word you say." I gave him a friendly smile. "I mean, come on. A respectable prosecutor down in your hood, asking you questions, threatening you? You really think they'll believe you over me?"

I could see the wheels turning in his head, and then something clicked. He reached into his back pocket and pulled out his phone. I'd been expecting this; anyone a little smarter would've thought of it three minutes ago, but one of the reasons I was here was because I'd read the kid's psych report. His IQ roughly matched that of a child's pencil case. Which was appropriate, because he was about as strong as a child's pencil. Before he even knew it was happening, I had his phone in my hand.

"I better confiscate that."

"Hey, fuck you, asshole."

I wagged a finger. "Now, now. Unless you want me to accidentally drop this down a drain, or better yet put some child porn on it, you're going to need to rethink your attitude."

We stared at each other for a few seconds, then he relented. The thing about kids, even dumb ones, is that they eventually realize when they're beaten. Alone, outwitted, weak, and looking at the guy who could mess up his future, Anton calmed himself. "So, fine. I know Bobby."

I leaned in. "I already know that, idiot. That's why I'm here. You're his best friend. What I don't know is where he is right now."

"I don't, either."

"Who do you live with?"

"My mom and sister."

"How old's your sister?"

His eyes narrowed again. "Why?"

I tried not to sigh. "Because, Anton, I want to know whether Bobby is hiding out in her bed."

"Oh. No, he's not. She's only eleven."

For a psychopathic kid on the run, the bed of an eleven-year-old was totally possible, assuming the mother didn't know. Which seemed unlikely.

"When did you last see him?" I asked.

"Sunday. I'm on paper, so I been going to school this week."

On paper. Why not just say on probation? I wondered. "It's two p.m. on Monday."

"Yeah, well, I went Thursday and Friday last week."

I wanted to congratulate him for knowing his days of the week but decided to stay on topic. "When you saw Bobby on Sunday, where was that?"

"Here."

"He came to the rec center?"

"Yeah, we always hang out here. Or meet here anyway."

"What time was that?"

"Lunchtime."

"And what did you guys do then?"

"We were just chillin', not doing anything much."

"Until when?" this was the vaguest and least-interesting timeline I'd ever assembled, but I needed Anton's best work.

He shrugged. "I don't know. Later."

"Later. Seriously?" My hands twitched, eager to choke the information out of him.

"Yeah. Like three. Maybe five."

"Where did he go then?"

"Home. He said he was going home."

"Who else was with you?"

"No one. Just us."

"Bullshit. I know there's three of you. Was Ledarius with you?"

Ledarius Williams. He was the one of this little triumvirate I'd not figured out. I knew who and what Bobby was. I knew the same about Anton, and that Bobby hung with this kid because it was like having a butler. Anton did anything and everything Bobby wanted him to. I know because I'd had friends like Anton growing up, kids who'd do your bidding even when they didn't want to, heck, when they didn't know they were doing it. Kids several bales short of a haystack who could be easily manipulated.

But Ledarius was different. He'd never been in our system, which for a kid who lived in this neighborhood and hung with these scallywags was stupefying. Either he was incredibly lucky, unbelievably smart, or an absolute saint. And I was pretty sure anyone who hung with Bobby was no saint, absolute or otherwise.

"Where does Ledarius stay?" I asked.

"I ain't snitching no more."

I took a deep breath. "Anton. Trust me when I say you've not snitched at all. You've been utterly useless. And telling me where one of your little buddies lives isn't snitching, it's saving me time. I can find that out easily enough, but I'm asking you because I don't have a lot of time, and I know that you know it's in your best interests to help me."

He looked at the ground and shuffled his feet. "You won't tell him I told you?"

"No, little man. I won't tell him you told me."

"He lives at the Cedar Brush Apartments. Building 2, number 113."

"I'm impressed you remember all those numbers."

He cocked his head, like he was unsure if I was actually impressed or making fun of him. Apparently he couldn't decide, because he didn't say anything for a moment, just nodded his head toward my hand. The one that held his phone.

"How do you afford an iPhone?" I asked.

"Stole it."

"Appreciate the honesty." I pushed the home sensor and the phone lit up. No security code. "I'll give your phone back," I said, "when I'm good and ready. Maybe the next time I see you in court."

"But I don't got a court date!" he protested.

"That's good; it means you're behaving yourself." I held up the phone. "Apart from theft and possession of stolen property, of course."

"You can't just take it."

"Why not? You did. And as law enforcement, I'm obliged to repatriate stolen property to its rightful owner."

"Do what?"

I sighed. "Where did you nick it from?"

"Nick it?"

"Steal. Where did you steal it from?"

"Here. Some guy playing basketball left it lying around."

"How careless."

"Right?" he said, as if I was on his side.

"Where's Ledarius now?"

"School, I 'spect."

"Even on a Monday?"

"Huh?" He scrunched up his face, my sarcasm skipping right by him.

"Does he go home after school?"

"No, we meet here usually. Me, him, an' Bobby."

"Splendid. Finally, useful information."

He didn't respond to that, just stared at me. "Where you from, anyway?"

"England. Know where that is?"

"Like, London?"

"Close enough. Now do me a favor and go home. Or school. Just get out of here for a while." *So I can meet Ledarius alone.*

He shrugged. "I gotta go home anyway. Sister's birthday. When can I have my phone back?"

"I'm not sure. I'll call you and let you know."

"OK. You better."

Call you on what? I wanted to scream. *You're a moron!* But instead I gave him my sweetest smile and said, "Thanks for your help today. I won't forget it."

He started to walk away, then stopped and turned. "Nick it." A slight smile twisted his lips. "I like that. I'm gonna use it."

"Help yourself," I muttered, giving him a good-bye wave.

I found a comfortable chair, one of four surrounding a coffee table covered with sports, car, and women's magazines. I picked up a *Cosmo* to read about heightening my man's orgasm, and waited for Ledarius.

O

I didn't like taking so much time off work, especially to spend it in a place like this, but it was interesting to me how anonymous I was there. I'd figured that a thirty-something white dude hanging out at the rec center in Austin's worst neighborhood would raise a few eyebrows. But I started to wonder whether perhaps this place was a safe zone amid all the gang turf wars, the police patrols, the ever-watching probation officers.

No one paid me any heed and I realized why Bobby, Ledarius,

and Anton came here. It was safe, yes, but more than that I wondered if this was a place where Bobby could let his guard down a little, not have to be the tough guy, the leader. Maybe Ledarius, too, though the idea of that trio having two leaders didn't make sense. I was curious to meet him.

His slim figure loped through the front door at three thirty, his head on a swivel as he looked around the large, main room. I recognized him right away; he was unusually tall for his age. Slender, too, with a very round and very black head that on the previous times I'd seen him sported a battered, black Chicago Bulls cap. Bill sideways, of course. He also wore heavy and thick glasses—I don't think I'd ever actually seen his eyes. I didn't like not being able to read someone's eyes.

He looked my way and seemed to hesitate before looking away again. I stood and walked over to him.

"Ledarius. Remember me?"

"Yeah," he said. I couldn't read his tone, and his eyes were pinpricks behind those lenses.

"Friend of Bobby's."

He shifted from one foot to the other, like he didn't approve of the word *friend*. "He here?" Ledarius asked.

"Not that I know of. I'm trying to find him, for his sister."

"That's what the cops said."

Now he had my attention. "Cops?"

"Yeah. Looking for him. Like you are."

"Not quite the same, I promise."

Those glasses were killing me; he was utterly expressionless. I decided to try a little honesty. "How come you've never been in the juvenile system?"

"Oh, right, cuz I'm black and live here."

"Pretty much. More 'cos you live here than 'cos you're black, though. All your friends are on paper." *There, I said it.*

"You don't know all my friends," he said, his voice still flat.

"I know some of them."

"Two."

"Both on paper."

Three teens wandered into the room, studiously ignoring us. Ledarius shifted on his feet so he could see them, though. "You judge people by the company they keep?"

It was an odd phrase for a kid like him to be using. Although, apparently, I didn't really know what sort of kid he was.

"Yes, I do. You don't?"

"Doesn't seem like that'd be fair, in my case."

"What do you mean?"

"I'm a kid. I live in the projects and go to school with other kids who live in the projects. I don't really get to choose the people around me like if I was an adult."

I nodded. "Good point."

"That's why I come here. Easier to pick who I chill with."

"People like Anton. He told me where you live, by the way." *Fuck you, Anton.*

Ledarius didn't seem surprised. "He's a good guy. Not saying he's the smartest, but . . ." For the first time a change in expression, the slightest of smiles, like he was embarrassed to be speaking that truth.

"Bobby a good guy?" I asked.

He was silent for a moment. "You should know."

Because I'm seeing his sister, or because he's like me? Which one, Ledarius? But of course I couldn't ask.

"He's a tough kid to understand," I said.

"He's dangerous," Ledarius said, matter-of-factly.

"In what way?"

"In any way he wants to be. You know that already. There's something off about him, something most people have but he doesn't."

Yeah, like a soul. Ledarius shrugged. "But he don't bother me none, we be cool."

"Do you know where he is?" I asked.

"Haven't seen him for a while. Like I told the cops."

"Since Sunday?"

That smile again. "Anton tell you that?"

"He did."

"Yeah, since Sunday."

"Cops say why they were looking for him?"

"Nope." He licked his lips and, I assumed, stared at me. "Pretty fucking obvious, though."

"It is?"

"That cop that got shot."

"Right. You know anything about that?"

"Shit, no." He held up his hands in surrender. "I don't smoke weed, boost cars, none of that. I ain't got no reason to kill a cop, shiiit." He dragged out that last word for a second or two.

"How about Bobby?"

"What about him?"

"Ledarius, dude, I'm trying to help him, not turn him in." Slight lie, that second part. "He said some stuff to me last week that made me . . . concerned."

"He said you guys got into it."

"Oh, he did?"

"Yeah." He dropped his backpack on the floor. "Look, man, you can't be telling him what he can and can't do. Don't you know that?"

"I'm not sure . . ." *I'm not sure how much he told you, and it better not be much.*

He lowered his voice. "Look, thing about Bobby. He likes to make his own decisions. No one can tell him shit, and if they try he either gets mad or acts like it was his idea in the first place. You tell him he's not capable or allowed to do something, that ain't good. All I know is, you got in his face about something to do with that cop and . . ." He looked around, but we were still just two people talking.

"You think he did it?"

"Shit, I don't know. He's capable. But I didn't think he was that dumb—not by a long shot. He knows what would happen."

"And yet here we are."

"Yeah," Ledarius conceded. "And Bobby ain't. I know what you're saying."

"Where would Bobby get a gun?"

"Honestly, that kid could get one anywhere he wanted. Talk it out of a cop's hand."

True enough. I suddenly wondered if he might just have gotten it from his sister. She'd never mentioned owning a gun, but then I'd never asked. And there she was, a beautiful woman in a small house on a rundown street, living alone with a teenage boy of questionable judgment. Having a gun would be a pretty smart move, which is to say *not* having one might not be. Maybe that was why she'd been cagey with me, defensive. Maybe her gun was missing.

"Look, I think you and I are on the same page," I said. "Help me find Bobby."

"I'm starting to think he's not a good influence." Again with the flat tone, I couldn't read this kid at all.

"Meaning?"

"Meaning, if he did this, he's not someone I need to be hanging out with."

"You don't have to. Just tell me where to find him."

"If he ain't with me or Anton, he be bouncing."

"Bouncing?"

"Yeah. He likes to mess with a couple of the gangs. Act like he's interested, then disappear on them."

"If he was trying to lay low, you think he might do that? Find some gangbangers to hang out with?"

He smiled again, and shook his head. "Mister, you sound like . . . just don't go asking for him talking like that."

"Like what?"

"*Gangbangers? Hanging out?* You'll get your ass whooped."

"Which gangs?"

"Depends on the moment. One day crabs, one day slobs."

"I have no idea what you're saying," I said, my patience wearing thin.

"Crabs are Crips, slobs are Bloods. The Pirus, that's Bloods to you, pimp in red. Crabs in blue." He nodded to the door. "Take a drive around and look. Just don't talk too much."

"So you have no idea where he is?"

"Nah, none."

"Can I give you my number in case he shows up?"

He shook his head. "I seen him do some stuff, man, but he never involved me. Ever. This one's a little too strong, ya know? Blowback from icing a cop's not something I need to be around to see, to feel. I work real hard to stay out of trouble, and it's washing up on my beach a little too close, you feel me?"

"Yeah, Ledarius, I feel you."

He picked up his backpack and started for the main door. "Peace out, man."

"I'm trying to," I said to his retreating back, then repeated it to myself. "I'm really trying to."

CHAPTER NINE

By the time Wednesday rolled around, Bobby was still missing and my special lady was disappearing from me. Most sisters, I presumed, would be frantic, calling the cops and running around town trying to find their missing brother, find out who was sheltering him. I knew he'd done this a few times before, just taken off to bed down with a friend. He did it to fuck with her, a show of power, something I'd done myself in the past. Her response wasn't what he expected, or wanted, and basically amounted to a shrug of the shoulders.

I wasn't sure if that was what she was doing this time, whether she was really worried about him but keeping it to herself, or whether she figured he was just being a dick and would come back. I suspected the former because she was more closed off than normal, short on the phone and not interested in coming over to my place, or watching me play my gigs.

For me, I was still anxious to find or hear from Bobby, although I was also relieved that the police didn't seem to be hot on his trail. I knew that they would be sooner or later—if nothing else, his PO would eventually notice a dead monitor battery or too many trips away from home. I wanted him back in the fold where I could take control of the situation, manage it the way I needed to.

Tension in the office was high, too. Terri Williams had been hauled over the coals for not preventing Ledsome from interviewing Bobby and other juveniles alone, without their lawyers. She hadn't known, of course; it wasn't her fault at all. But a murder investigation shines a bright light on everything it touches, and if a corner of your house is dirty then people notice. And when those people aren't getting anywhere with catching their killer, pointing fingers at other people's faults is a handy distraction.

Also, McNulty had been in and out all week. Apparently he'd been shitting so much from Curra's that he'd become dehydrated. He'd tried coming to work a couple of times, more worried about his judge application than his job, I'm sure, but pretty soon turned pale and staggered back to his car.

Which I didn't appreciate, because it meant I had to cover his cases for him.

I was looking over his docket when my office phone rang.

"Dominic, this is Judge Portnoy. Do you have a moment before court to stop by?"

"Of course, Judge. Is this about a specific case? If so, I can grab a public defender so we're not ex parte."

"No, no," she said. "Nothing like that, more of a personal matter. I just wanted to get your opinion on something."

I hesitated, my mind in overdrive trying to figure out what she wanted. Music related? That judge position? "I'll be right there, Your Honor," I said. I rose and checked my tie in the mirror, grabbed my jacket, and walked out of the DA's offices, through the main section of the Betts, and into the part of the building where court administration was housed, and where the judges had their offices.

Portnoy's was the largest, of course, being the only elected district judge. I knocked on her door and she opened it herself, standing to one side as she beckoned me in.

"Have a seat," she said.

She was a tall woman in her early fifties, with long blond hair that was starting to gray and a face that was a little too narrow to be attractive. Maybe when she was young and with a good dose of makeup, but now she just looked the way she acted in court—a little harsh.

"How can I help?" I asked as she rounded her desk and sat opposite me.

"It's somewhat sensitive, to be honest." She rested her elbows on the desk and clenched her hands together, almost hiding behind her fists. "Like I said, a personal matter."

"Well, I should probably start by promising that whatever you tell me goes nowhere," I said sincerely. "You have my word."

"Thank you, I appreciate that." She gave a tight smile. "Here's the situation. A friend of mine received an envelope with her name on it. Someone had slid it under her office door. In that envelope was a disk."

"A disk?"

"With video on it. About fifteen seconds of video of her having . . . relations with someone other than her husband."

"Ah, I see."

"Yes," she said.

"Was there a note or anything with the video?"

"Like a blackmail note?" she asked.

"Yes, asking for money."

"No, just the video." Portnoy sat back in her chair. "As you might imagine, my friend doesn't want to call the police."

"I can see why. Once they're involved, there's no way to keep that quiet. I mean, I'm sure they'd try, but if it went to trial your friend would have to testify, the tape would be played . . ."

"And that would be the end of her marriage and her career," Portnoy said.

"Does your friend have any idea who it might be? Or what they might want?"

"Maybe. That's why she asked for my help, and I'm asking for yours."

"Of course. As long as it's nothing illegal, which I'm sure you wouldn't—"

"No, no, of course not," she said hurriedly. She cleared her throat. "So, the video relates to an incident in which the police were called to her house."

I was confused. "Sorry, Judge, I thought you said it was video of her and—"

"It is. It's complicated, some bad luck and bad timing. Anyway, she thinks that someone who was there is taking advantage of those circumstances."

"You said the police were there." I frowned, thinking. "I could print you a copy of the incident report. Would that help?"

"Precisely my thinking, Counselor. I think that's the best place to start. And thank you."

"Sure, I'll do it right now. Give me ten or fifteen minutes." I stood. "Can you tell me the date and the address, so I can find the right report?"

She opened a drawer and pulled out a pad of paper. She wrote on the top page and tore it off. "That's the date, time, and address," she said, then paused before continuing. "I imagine you'll notice a few of the details, as any curious person might."

"I'll try hard not to," I said.

"I think that's a little unrealistic," she said. "But please don't share with anyone else, and throw that piece of paper away when you're done. As you'll see, the address is mine."

I walked to the door, opened it, and turned back to her. "Judge, I have no idea what's on the tape or in the offense report. But of all people in this world, I know that people make mistakes, show lapses in judgment. And as I hope you've seen from the way I practice law here in the juvenile courts, I believe that everyone deserves a second chance, and that no one should have their life defined, or ruined, by one incident."

Her voice was a whisper. "Thank you, Dominic. I appreciate that."

"Give me fifteen minutes, Judge, and I'll have that report for you."

"Thank you."

I stood there for a second, a thought striking me. "I just realized something. Every time we log into Versadex, which is where we get the reports, it's noted. Like, I can't do it anonymously." She looked at me, obviously not quite getting it, so I went on. "Well, Judge, I can only assume whoever sent that is going to blackmail you, or try, even if they haven't done so yet."

"And?"

"If this does somehow blow up, if people do find out—"

"No one's going to find out," she said emphatically.

"You can't promise me that any more than I can promise you the same thing," I said, my voice firm. I'd seen firsthand the cleverest of schemes unravel. "Look, all I'm asking is that you send me an e-mail requesting that I pull this report. That way there's a record that I was trying to help you, not do anything underhanded. It's a matter of timing, me digging around before anything's known, it could look bad. I'm trying to help you out here, Judge, I really am. But I can't afford to put myself at risk."

She thought for a moment. "OK, I guess that's fair."

When I got to my desk, I sat and waited. It didn't take long for her e-mail to pop into my inbox.

Dominic, I wonder if I might ask a quick favor. There was an incident at an address in Legend Oaks last Thursday. A friend was involved and may need legal counsel, but I can't know that until I see the police report. If you could pull it for me, I'd be grateful. Specifics below . . .

Short, sweet, and to the point.

I typed the information, the date and the address, into Versadex. The screen that came up puzzled me, though, because there was no report. Just an incident number entered by the patrol officer, one Fernando Chipelo. Also uploaded was the dash-cam video and body-cam from all three officers. Which would include, I assumed, the revealing footage on Judge Portnoy's disk that I planned to look at later.

Although maybe not. If a record was kept, if it showed me downloading it . . . the impulsive me burned to do it, to download and watch it and later find an explanation, an excuse, for having done so. I took some deep breaths and tried to see the bigger picture, though, instead picking up the phone and dialing the APD/DA's liaison officer.

Chad Anders had been doing that job for three years, a bubbly, friendly guy who looked like a kid even though he was nearing fifty. There wasn't a man alive who responded faster to e-mails or requests for information.

"Chad, Dominic here."

"Hey, man, what's up?"

"I need to talk to one of your guys. Patrol officer named Fernando Chipelo. Asap."

"Sure, I'll get hold of him now, have him call you. At the office?"

"Or you could just give me his cell number."

"Man, you don't quit, do you?" He chuckled. "Never have, never will, but feel free to keep asking."

"I will. And yes, I'll be in my office."

It took ten minutes, but Chipelo called. "How can I help you, sir?"

"I was looking into something that happened on your shift a week ago. Thursday evening, to be precise. I have an incident number, but there's no report."

"Oh. What was the incident, sir? We don't write reports for everything, but maybe I'll remember."

"When do you not write a report?" I was wondering if someone had told him not to.

"When the call turns out to be a dud, most often. We get a lot of calls that wind up being nothing, just a contact with a member of the public. We'll make a note in our system but not write a report."

"So why an incident number?"

"That's generated on the front end, as soon as a call comes in— it's automatic. That way we have a number to give to someone, that member of the public, in case they want to call back and make another statement or reference the incident somehow."

"I'm guessing you'll remember this incident," I said.

"Oh yes?"

"You went to a house, went inside, and found a respectable member of our community in a compromising position."

A pause on his end. "Yes, sir. I recall that."

"I'm seeing no report on it, but some video footage uploaded."

"We're required to do that, sir." He sounded a little defensive.

"Did you watch the video?"

"No, sir. I mean, I didn't need to, I was there to see it in person."

"And the other two officers, they saw it all?"

"Just Officer De Jong. He had a rookie with him who was at the back of the house."

I took out a pen and paper. "That rookie knew what you'd seen, right?"

"Yes, sir." He didn't elaborate, but I was sure they all had a good chuckle.

"Officer De Jong's first name?"

"Are we in trouble, sir?"

"No, not in the slightest. It's just a delicate situation; I'm trying to save someone from further embarrassment."

"The lady?"

"Right. Did you happen to know who she was?"

"No, sir. Once we realized what was going on, we excused

ourselves pretty quickly. And she made it clear she didn't want us sticking around, if you know what I mean."

I gave a gentle laugh. "Can't blame her, eh?"

"No, sir, not at all. And it's Nick De Jong."

"Thanks. The rookie's name?"

"Ernesto Robles."

"Thank you. I really appreciate the cooperation. The lady in question just wants to make sure this doesn't get out; I don't expect you'll be bothered over this anymore."

"I felt really bad, sir. We only went in because we thought someone was in her house. Illegally. We didn't mean to embarrass her."

"She knows that. She doesn't blame you at all."

"I'm glad to hear that." He sounded genuinely relieved. "Anything else I can help you with, sir?"

"No, that's all. Thanks." I reached for the button to disconnect, but heard his voice again.

"Sir? You still there?"

"Yep, I'm here. What's up?"

"It totally slipped my mind, and I don't know if it makes any difference to anything."

"What's that?"

"Well," he said. "I had a rider that night. Guy from your office, actually. He'd have seen everything on the computer. Our body cams feed directly to it; so if he was watching, he'd have seen what we saw."

"Is that so?" Something bubbled inside me, a mix of surprise, relief, and shock, but mostly amusement.

"Yes, sir. You need his name, too?"

"No, that's OK," I said. "I know who you're talking about." *Brian fucking McNulty. Wannabe judge, general irritation, and now voyeur.*

And, most interestingly, he'd not said a word to me about it.

CHAPTER TEN

The following afternoon, Thursday, I called Brian at home. "Feeling any better?"

"Sometimes. Mostly not."

"You should go see a doctor."

"No, I'm just dehydrated," he said. "Don't want to drag myself down there, pay the thirty-dollar co-pay, and sit in the waiting room full of sick people, only to be told to lay on the couch and drink water." He coughed weakly. "Fuck that."

"You need me to bring you anything?"

"Nah, Connie has me covered. She's a good nurse, that one."

"Cool," I said. "Hey, did you remember to cancel your ride-out for tonight?"

"Oh, shit, no. Dammit, thanks for the reminder."

"Well, I can do that for you."

"You can? Wow, thanks Dom. I wrote the sergeant's name on the white board in our office. They usually come by for me around four, four-thirty."

"I'm on it. Rest up, see you next week."

"Yeah, I won't be in tomorrow. Thanks again."

I rang off and looked at the clock. Ten minutes to four. I closed my office door and changed out of my suit, pulling on jeans and my official DA windbreaker. I checked that I had my wallet and phone, then walked past Terri's office. Her door was open so I stuck my head in.

"I'm taking Brian's spot tonight."

"What do you mean?"

"Riding out. I called earlier to check on him, and he forgot to cancel with APD, so I said I'd fill in, unless you have an objection."

"No," she said. "Nothing much going on tomorrow, so I'll cover whatever we have. Enjoy the ride and take tomorrow off. Which sector is it?"

"Henry."

"I thought he covered David."

"I wanted a little more excitement; thought I'd ring the changes just for tonight. I cleared it with both sergeants."

"Fine with me." She chuckled. "Henry Sector. Have your own vest?"

"No."

"Then don't forget to duck." She smiled. "See ya on Monday, if you ain't dead."

I grinned. "If I am, cover my docket for me."

At four o'clock sharp, a black-and-white police Crown Vic bumped into the parking lot in front of the Betts and circled around to the step where I was sitting. The officer, a Hispanic man who looked to be in his mid-thirties, threw me a wave and then got out and came around the car to greet me.

"You're my prosecutor, sir?"

I stood. "Dominic, none of that *sir* nonsense."

He smiled. "Oh, sure. I'm Thiago DeAraujo. Call me Thiago." We shook hands. "Hey, are you that British prosecutor? You were all over the news a year or so ago, I recognize you now."

"One and the same." I gave him a friendly wink. "But don't say British, I'm English."

"Not the same thing?"

"It'd be like calling a Canadian a North American. Not quite specific enough."

"Or like calling me, a Brazilian, South American. Got you." He jerked a thumb at the car. "You ready to go?"

When we were seated, I asked, "So how long have you been with APD?"

"Nine years," he said. "Senior guy on the shift. You ever ride out before?"

"Yeah, a dozen times maybe. I usually get out at all the calls, except the traffic stops." Those were the most unpredictable. Pretty much every other call you knew what you were headed to, and other cops were likely there already, but several officers had told me they prefer to worry solely about the driver they're pulling over, rather than the driver *and* me.

"That works. Otherwise, get out whenever you want, just stay here if I ask you to."

"Will do."

"And you know where the button is for the AR? Ever shot one?"

"I do and I have. Maybe if things get a little slow I can fire it out the window a few times."

He grinned. "Yeah, I'm sure no one would mind."

"So we're off to Henry Sector?"

"Yeah, one of the spicier parts of town." He put the car in drive and we set off. I looked at the computer that sat between us, with the calls listed. "Nothing happening right now, so maybe we'll run traffic, or just back other people up. But don't worry, the quiet never lasts long."

As we drove east, we talked and he told me about himself. A Brazilian who moved to Boston and then Austin, he was still in the Navy Reserves, and was desperately in love with his blond, Minnesotan wife, a nurse. I knew because his face lit up when he talked about her and, for the thousandth time, I wondered what it was like to feel such love and passion for another person.

Don't get me wrong, I do feel emotion when I meet a girl. It's just a little more, how can I put this? A little more me-oriented. For example, I get sort of obsessed and doting, jealous even, until I'm suddenly not. My current situation was different, had lasted longer than usual, but partly that was because she played hard to get. She wasn't fooled by me, didn't let me manipulate her. I respected that. My mind lingered on her a moment, then shifted inevitably to Bobby, and I made myself focus on the task at hand: Henry Sector.

For patrol purposes, the Austin Police Department divided Austin into nine sectors. The smallest was the downtown area, George Sector, where half the cops rode bikes. Below George lay David Sector, the largest, which covered the most affluent part of the city, its southwest corner. Extending directly east, with the always-packed Interstate 35 as its western border, lay Henry, a part of town I was not familiar with. I soon saw why.

It seemed a world apart from downtown Austin, ruled by its predictable, gridded streets and familiar landmarks. Different, too, from the wide-open but ordered David, where the apartment complexes were properly kempt and so many people lived safely in their gated, or at least community-watched, neighborhoods.

No, right from the get-go I could see that this part of Austin was different. The roads themselves wound up and down through neighborhoods that were hard to distinguish from each other because the small patches of undeveloped land were littered with the tarps of the homeless and small clusters of blacks or Hispanics who stood stock-still and watched intently as we passed by. The apartment complexes here were devoid of trees and swimming pools, five-hundred-dollar-a-month shitboxes stacked on top of each other and home to more people than you'd want visiting, let alone living, in your Westlake McMansion.

"See this bus stop coming up?" Thiago said. "Watch them scatter like cockroaches when we go by."

The bus stop sat on a side street by the parking lot of a convenience store, and Thiago slowed to turn right into the lot. Six men and two women looked up, spotting us seemingly in unison, and without hesitation they split up, striding away in different directions, with their hands in their pockets. They might as well have been whistling innocently, as guilty as they obviously were.

"Buying and selling drugs?" I asked.

"Drugs for sure. Probably guns, too. Pisses the community off. Folks don't feel safe catching the bus, and that's how most people here get to work. I come down here a couple times a shift to scare them off, but they scuttle right back."

"Like cockroaches."

"Precisely."

"Speaking of which, I'm curious. What's your opinion of us prosecutors?" I asked.

"You really wanna know?" He glanced over, smiling. "I'm kidding. Don't have much interaction with you guys, to be honest. Occasional phone call or e-mail complaining about something we screwed up."

"Then don't screw things up," I said, smiling back so he'd know I was kidding. "How about testifying?"

"Twice in nine years. Now, I've been to juvie court a few times, but the case always got postponed."

"Yeah, that happens. Usually because the kid doesn't show up for court."

"So why do you let them out before their trial?"

"I don't," I said. "That's the judge's call. They rarely hold kids in detention, not unless they're some kind of danger to society."

"Far as I can tell," he said, "a lot of them are, and you still let them go."

"Like I said. Not me, the judges."

"We joke about it," he said. "We catch them and bring them in, you give them hugs and lollipops and let them go."

"You're not far wrong. It can be frustrating for us, too, but we do the best we can."

Just after nine, Thiago pulled into a gas station. "Bathroom break. Only about three in this sector clean enough, and welcoming enough, for us to use," he said.

"That's a shame." We climbed out of the car and once my door was shut, he locked up and we walked to the main doors.

"Tell me about it. I drive out of sector to eat; pretty much every fast-food and burger joint here is manned by ex-cons or juveniles on probation." He winked. "I don't need extra toppings on my sandwich, if ya get my drift."

"I sure do." I held the gas-station door open for him. "And neither do I."

He let me use the restroom first, and I wrinkled my nose as I did so. If this was one of the clean ones, I could see why he avoided the others. I flushed and washed my hands, then walked out to the car to wait. Leaning on the cruiser, I made a phone call.

Thiago reappeared a minute later, a serious look on his face. "We gotta go. Some juveniles trespassing in an abandoned house."

As I climbed into the car, I groaned dramatically. "Juveniles? Didn't I make that a rule?"

"What's that?"

"I see enough of the little buggers during the day, I think I deserve a night off from them."

He laughed as he switched on the overhead lights and siren. "Too late," he said. "Buckle up, we're the closest ones to the house, so for once you could be catching kids instead of letting them go."

I tried to keep an eye on the road names, but daylight was fading and half of the streetlights were out. I followed along as we turned right from Montopolis Drive onto Riverside, the police car's tires squealed as Thiago cut off a corner into a smaller, residential street, and then I was lost.

"Who called this in?" I asked, above the wail of the siren.

"A neighbor, I'm guessing." He glanced at the computer. "Doesn't give a name, and you see how it says *DNC* at the end?"

"Yes. Do Not Contact, right?"

"You *have* ridden out before," he said with a smile. "So I'm guessing a neighbor who doesn't want to be seen talking to the cops. Pretty common around here."

Thiago killed the lights and siren a couple of blocks from the target house. He turned on the spotlight by his window, directing it onto the houses as we cruised down the street, looking for the right number. He stopped several houses away and shone the light on the address we'd been given. The house was small, its postage stamp of a front yard overgrown, and the chain-link fence around it rusted and broken. The windows weren't broken, though, and I couldn't see any movement behind them.

"We waiting for backup?" I asked.

He looked at the computer. "No one close. Probably just a bunch of kids smoking weed and drinking. You wanna stay here? They might run."

"No, I'll come. I could use some exercise."

He opened the glove compartment. "Spare flashlight, grab it. If the place is abandoned, there'll be no electricity."

"Thanks." I grabbed the flashlight and followed him out of the car and along the sidewalk toward the house. The street was quiet; if the kids were in there partying, they weren't very good at it. Or maybe they'd passed out, but nine o'clock seemed a little early for that. Even for kids.

The gate to the property was open, hanging off one hinge, and I let him lead me up the short path to the porch. The boards on it sagged, and I wasn't convinced we wouldn't fall through, so I waited as Thiago stepped up to the front door. He paused there and spoke into his radio.

"Henry 507. The door's open. I don't hear anything, so they probably took off. I'll check the place and advise."

He held the flashlight in his left hand and put his right on the butt of his gun.

"You want me to wait out here?" I asked.

"Probably should."

I watched Thiago disappear inside the house and saw the beam of his flashlight bobbing up and down through the front window. I turned to look down the street, but all the doors were closed, no nosy neighbors wondering what was going on. In three minutes, Thiago came out and spoke into his radio. "Henry 507. Code four." *All clear.*

"Nothing?" I asked.

"A few cans and a lot of cigarette butts. You wanna see inside an abandoned house?"

"Sure." I stepped onto the porch and went through the front door. Thiago followed me. "Smells of mold and weed," I said.

"But nothing recent."

"There's a dead animal in here somewhere," I said, wrinkling my nose.

"Probably a rat in the wall or attic. Raccoon, maybe."

I shone my flashlight around the tiny living room, brushing it over two armchairs and a long couch, all in brown. A coffee table knelt in front of the couch, two of its legs broken off, the chipped wood surface sloping down to the beige, stained carpet. Crumpled beer cans littered the floor, and a hub cap had been turned into a giant ashtray, one that hadn't been emptied in a while.

A door led into the kitchen, all Formica and broken cupboards. The fridge had fallen forward, propped up now by a dusty kitchen counter. I turned and walked back through the living room to the lone bedroom. A double bed held a mattress and nothing else, and I grimaced at the stains on it. As desperate for sex as teenagers got, would they really drape themselves over that? I hoped not. Another mattress stood against the far wall, between the windows and the closet, resting at an angle like a teepee.

Something caught my eye when my light flickered over the base of the mattress. A shoe. I looked again, wondering whether one of the hoodlums was hiding out, or maybe passed out. I shifted to my right to make sure the shoe hadn't just been left behind, but there was definitely a leg attached.

I cleared my throat. "Hey, Thiago."

"Yeah?" he called from the living room.

"I want to show you something."

"I got enough porn at home, thanks."

"No, really."

I watched as the beam from his flashlight preceded him into the room. "What's up?" he asked.

I pointed my light at the mattress, and after a moment he saw it, too. He slowly drew his weapon, and I backed up a little, giving him room, my eyes fixed on that one, unmoving shoe.

"Austin Police," Thiago said. "Show yourself."

We waited, but there was no movement. Thiago gestured for me to step farther back, so I did. The room was silent but for his breathing and the creak of his gun belt as he shifted. He spoke again: "Austin Police, show yourself."

He moved forward toward the mattress, then seemed to realize he couldn't move it while holding his gun and flashlight, so I stepped toward him, training my light on the mattress. allowing him to holster his flashlight and have a free hand. I stood close behind so he could pull the top of the mattress from the wall, and he did so with a flick of his wrist, his gun aimed squarely at whoever was behind it. The mattress fell to the floor with a whump, kicking up dust that made us cover our mouths.

The body sat there, legs crossed like he'd died doing yoga, his back against the wall and his hands resting gently in his lap. His skin was sallow, a mix of gray and yellow that told me he'd been dead a few days. A gun lay on the floor beside his right knee, and a single, spent shell casing sat upright less than a foot away, as if someone had placed it there on purpose.

Thiago spoke into his radio. "Henry 507. We have a sig three. White male, looks like single gunshot wound to the head." Then he turned to me. "We need to leave everything as we found it, and wait for Homicide to get down here."

I backed out of the room, unable to take my eyes off the body, off the neat hole in the right side of his head, the patch of red on the wall behind him, and the ragged, tangled mess of hair and bone where the bullet had exited. I made sure not to touch anything in the living room, heading straight for the front door, which was still open. Outside, the fresh air hit me, and I almost gagged, which surprised me. Thiago took it as a sign of emotion and put a hand on my shoulder.

"Sorry you had to see that, man," he said.

"Hey, no worries. I guess the fresh air is bad for me."

He gave a gentle laugh. "Yeah, something like that." He held up a finger as the dispatcher spoke into his earpiece. "Negative," he replied. "No visible wallet or sign of an ID. I didn't touch the body. Ten-four, will wait for Homicide."

We stood in silence for a moment, looking up and down the street. "Crime Scene guys on the way?" I asked, more to pass the time than anything. Of course they were.

"Yeah. They'll do their thing, maybe find out who he is."

"If it helps, I can tell you that right now."

His head snapped up. "You know him?"

"Yes," I said. "His name's Robert something, and he's a fifteen-year-old juvenile delinquent. His sister and probation officer know him as Bobby."

CHAPTER ELEVEN

We stuck around for another two hours. Thiago and several other officers were sent to knock on doors to find out if anyone had seen or heard anything, but in this neighborhood everyone knew that was a fool's errand. Four of the twenty houses on the street were as abandoned as this one, and the homes that were occupied contained either old people too deaf or blind to see anything, or scraggly-limbed drug users who wouldn't have noticed if a Russian tank had driven down the street and blasted Bobby into smithereens.

I lingered on the scene for a couple of reasons. Mostly I didn't want to have to tell his sister what we'd found. *Whom* we'd found, sorry. This was one of those times when I looked closely inside myself and tried to feel something. For her sake, but also as a test of my own condition; because if there was one kid I should feel bad about being killed, it was Bobby. Yeah, he'd been impetuous, stupid, and headstrong, and he ignored my advice, but he couldn't help any of that, just like I couldn't help being the way I am. And I'd wanted to help him, to help his sister. Get him into adulthood, for fuck's sake—that at least.

Two detectives headed up the investigation, best I could tell, and I didn't know either of them. That didn't matter, I walked right up and introduced myself. They'd want a statement from me as one of the two people who'd found him, but they might also like having a prosecutor on scene, just in case.

"We've been looking for this kid," the male detective said. "Found his GPS monitor in a drainage ditch a few days ago; he must've cut it off. His probation officer had no clue where he was. Anyway, we're waiting for Sergeant Brannon to get here."

"This has to do with Detective Ledsome's murder?" I asked.

"Well, let's just say Brannon was real interested in talking to this kid about it."

"Damn. I guess it makes sense. . . . They said a kid shot her. This kid?"

"Maybe." He nodded toward the house. "And looks like he decided he didn't want to face the music."

"You're thinking suicide?" I asked.

"Gun's next to the body, one shot in the head. Seems like a fair bet, but we'll look into it."

"What about the disturbance call, people being in the house?" No one seemed to care about that anymore.

The cop laughed. "Probably a few kids looking to get high, stumbled in there and saw him tucked behind his mattress and took off. Long gone by now and hardly our biggest problem." His face went serious. "Unless they contaminated the crime scene. Goddamned kids."

I leaned against the hood of Thiago's car, which was nice and warm with the engine still running, and thought about it. Suicide. I supposed it was possible, if unlikely. Generally, the things that drive people to kill themselves don't exist in people like me and Bobby. Guilt, remorse, pessimism about the future. Put another way, we're the center of our own universes, and everyone else's, in our minds, and so why would we destroy the only thing on the planet that matters: us? My life had gotten pretty shitty a few times, but I'd never considered biting down on the end of a gun barrel, not once. I'd be happy for others to die to make my life better; that wouldn't bother me in the slightest, but to take my own life? Not that.

On the other hand, the things that prevent empaths from killing themselves are absent with us, too. We wouldn't care about devastating friends and family, nor do we have any religious compunctions holding us back. And there's our impulsiveness. Right there, a drive toward impetuous, dumb behavior could have been enough to make Bobby pull the trigger. An idiotically irreversible swipe at me for telling him what he could and couldn't do, maybe even at his sister. The gifts of foresight and an awareness of consequences are not our best traits, especially when young. And a reckless kid who knows he's going to prison for the rest of his life . . .

Whatever happened to Bobby, I figured his sister would likely blame me, or at the very least prefer some time alone. For me, I get bored alone and could use the distraction, the entertainment that comes with bullying a lesser human being. Well, I should rephrase: bullying an actual human being. I called Brian McNulty, wondering just how much he wanted to be my friend.

BRIAN

"It's late, Dom. I was going to bed." Me in my pajamas when Dom came calling, it was becoming a theme.

"Feeling better?" he asked.

"Much, thanks. Still a little tired, but I may actually head into work tomorrow."

"Glad to hear it."

"Where are you?"

"That's partly why I'm calling," he said. "I forgot to cancel your ride-along, so I just took your place. I'm out with them now."

Like a cuckoo, was my first thought. "That's OK. Having fun?"

"You know. A nice mix of excitement and boredom. Pleasant change from the office, though, no doubt about that."

"Oh, so I guess you'll be off tomorrow," I said.

"Yep. Figured I better let you know what I was doing, so Terri or someone else didn't tell you, worry you that I was stealing your job."

"I appreciate that, but I don't think I'd have jumped to that conclusion." *Except it was my first thought. Not very nice of me.*

"So, dude, I've been thinking. That poker party may not be a good idea."

My heart sank. "Why not?"

"Sometimes when we play, we get a little crazy."

"Like what?"

"Well, here's the thing. You and I, we've not been close friends or anything. I'm pretty private, so my fault. But we respect each other, right?"

"Yeah, Dom, sure. Absolutely."

"It's just that I'd hate for that to go away, for something to spoil that. Especially with you about to be a judge."

"We're just playing for fun, the money isn't related to the poker. I get that, it's not a problem."

"Oh, no," Dominic said. "It's not that at all. Like I said, sometimes we cut loose a little."

Something, to be entirely honest, I have a very hard time doing because I worry a lot about what people think of me. In the past, Dominic's called me uptight, and I'd have to say that he's right. That's part of why I want the judge job so much, I think: people will respect me more, at least I'll be a little more confident.

"Dom, I promise. Unless you're doing cocaine or hiring prostitutes, I'm game." *And maybe even then*, I thought to myself. *Maybe.*

"Well, I guess I can let you make the call." He laughed, like he was a little embarrassed. "I just don't want you to think less of me for even suggesting this."

"I promise, I won't."

"All right, then." He took a breath. "So, like I said. We get a little crazy. Very. And the thing is, we all have high-pressure jobs, responsible jobs. We're all single, or at least unmarried. And way too old to be doing crazy shit, so we make sure we just do it together and not in public."

"What happens at poker stays at poker," I said.

"Yeah, precisely. Maybe you do get it."

"Dom, it's OK, I do. And I feel like you're already making excuses, but I'm not gonna judge you." The truth was, I loved that he was opening up to me like this. I wanted him to tell me something nuts, something extreme. I wanted whatever it was to shock the hell out of me.

"Fine," he said. "I'll cut to the chase. We have themes for each card game. Like, we all have significant others, so one weekend we all had to show each other pictures of our ladies naked."

"Oh, man, like candid shots?"

"Yeah, exactly."

"Connie would kill me! But yeah, I'm with you."

"That's why it was candid; I don't think any of our girls would've gone for it. Anyway, this next game it's Russian roulette."

"Whoa, seriously?"

"Yes and no. We're not going to use a gun, spin the chamber. Nothing like that, we don't have a death wish."

"So how does it work?"

"Each of us has to bring something, then we draw lots to see who does what challenge."

"Like what?" I asked, intrigued.

"I don't want to give it all away, just give you an idea. So the thing I have to bring is a paintball gun. They have them like revolvers, so whoever ends up with it will wear a paintball mask, spin the chamber, and maybe shoot themselves in the face."

"That could still hurt. A lot."

"Right?" he said. "But no permanent damage. I thought of that one." He sounded proud, and it did seem a little extreme, but without being lethal.

"So what would mine be?"

"Last man in always gets the worst assignment," he said, but lightly like it wouldn't be that bad.

"I'm listening."

"You have to bring a benzo, one that's used as a treatment for anxiety. Whoever ends up taking it will be fucking hilarious."

"Oh." We saw kids with benzos all the time, usually snagged from their parents. Using them was against the law if they weren't specifically prescribed for you. And even though I hated to, I knew I had to draw the line there. A prospective judge couldn't be breaking the law. Apart from maybe a prostitute, and the truth is I've always wondered what that'd be like. But not drugs. "Dom, I'm sorry, I can't do that."

"Do what?"

"Illegally provide drugs. Possess them, even. Ask me to do something else."

"It's not my call, and everyone has their job. This is yours."

I didn't like doing this on the phone, I wanted to look at him, try to read his eyes. He didn't seem like the kind of guy who took orders from others, but then I didn't know his friends, who or what they were. I sure wanted to find out, though.

"A prospective judge can't be dealing drugs, Dom, you know that. Something else, ask your friends."

"It's not dealing drugs, not even close. You'll obtain them legally, and since you're not selling them, there's nothing illegal about it."

"How about I bring along a prostitute."

Dom laughed. "Where the hell would you get one of those? One of the scrubbers from South Congress? Backpage.com?"

"I don't know." I didn't, and I felt stupid for suggesting it. "Anything but drugs."

I could hear the smile in his voice. "And some HIV-riddled whore is your 'anything but'?"

"I was just trying to think outside the box," I said.

"Well, don't. In or out, matey; I'm sorry, but you play by the rules or you don't play at all."

"But—"

"No," he snapped. "The new guy doesn't get to change the rules. You need to make a decision." His tone softened. "Like I said before, it's a specific drug and you can get it legally. You won't be breaking the law, Brian."

"How about I give you the money, pay for it, and you get them. You know, since you know what we need and all that."

The moment I said those words, I was disappointed in myself. I sounded like a coward trying to get someone else to do something I was too chicken to do. Not *sounded like*, that's exactly what was happening. I'm pretty sure I went down in his estimation when I said that, and I know I went down in mine.

But it's funny. When Dominic mentioned the two-grand buy in, that seemed like a big deal at the time. I mean, it's a lot of money still; but it's *my* money, and I can do what I want with it, pretty much. Legally speaking. But drugs are different, and I wasn't convinced he was telling the truth about the legality of buying and providing benzos, even if he had a particular brand or whatever in mind.

If it was so easy and legal, why was it the worst task, the one given to the new guy?

So I had to decide, and from the way he sounded, I had to decide right there and then. Not my strength. I thought about the judge position, the responsibility of that job not just while I wore the robe but in conducting myself off the bench. The way I acted, the way I spoke to people, the way I comported myself in my day-to-day activities. Playing in high-stakes poker games kind of went with the old-fashioned image of a judge with his buddies, smoking cigars and swirling whiskey in crystal glasses. *That* I was fine with. Kinda cool, actually. But judges didn't go buying drugs from who-knows-where and handing them around, taking them to some kind of Russian roulette game that unknown people, probably under-employed musicians, devised for their amusement.

Whiskey is one thing, drugs quite another.

Problem was, I wanted something else just as much as that robe. I wanted to be Dominic's friend. I wanted to be someone he invited to these get-togethers, to do wild and slightly crazy things with long-haired hipster musicians who toked Mary Jane while I turned a blind eye and they told inappropriate jokes. I wanted that judge job, yes, but I'd lived too much of my life isolated, without close friends. Certainly, without close *cool* friends. Taking that robe would be a step away from cool, Dom's kind of cool anyway, a step away from being fun and reckless and getting stupid on Saturday nights.

Plus, I wasn't a judge yet. Not even close, and maybe I wouldn't be.

I knew this would be my last chance to grab that lifeline, to be someone other than the square, responsible, likeable Brian McNulty. Judge Brian McNulty, even. Same ordinary guy with a slightly shinier pen.

And in that moment, I wanted one thing more than I wanted the other. Just for once. Just *this* once.

"You said a specific benzo?" I asked. "A legal one."

"Yeah, it's called Flunitrazepam."

"Never heard of it."

"That's probably a good sign."

"Wait, if it's legal . . . why would you say that if—"

"Take a breath, Brian, for heaven's sake. It's legal, I'm messing with you."

I did take a breath. "Can you text me the name?"

"Flunitrazepam," he said again. "Spelled the usual way. Just Google it. It'll have to come from Mexico or Canada, so do it soon."

"Oh. You're sure it's legal?"

"The only thing I'm sure of is that you're a broken record. I already said it was." I heard the smile in his voice. "That is, if you get it from abroad."

"Abroad?"

"Yeah, you know. Foreign countries. Abroad."

"I don't understand." I didn't. Was I supposed to travel to Mexico or something?

"It's pretty simple. It's illegal to *sell* it here in the US. It's legal to buy it, which means you get it from somewhere that *isn't* the US."

"How?"

"Jesus, Brian, do I have to do this for you? Online."

The last seconds, the final chance to pull out, tell him it was too much hassle, too dangerous, too stupid. Tell him whatever, maybe that I just didn't want to do it. Tell him, now or never.

"OK," I said. "I'm in. Online it is."

"Good chap. Hey, I better run, we're on the move."

He hung up, and I felt a surge of pride. Not only was Dominic including me in his poker game, his *high-stakes* poker game, but I was also in on their special dare. I wondered for a moment who else would be there, but I had absolutely no idea. Musicians? Movers and shakers? Cool people, to be sure. Maybe even people who could help me get that judgeship. He did say that they all had high-pressure, responsible jobs. It felt like I'd wangled an invitation to a private club, and that had never happened to me. Ever.

CHAPTER TWELVE

THE GIRL WITH THE LIME-GREEN DRESS

I was never under any illusion as to who Dominic was, any more than I doubted my own brother's hollow nature. I had an inkling as to how my brother saw *me*, though, there was that difference. Dominic? Harder to read.

When I first saw him, I was at a bus stop, wearing a green dress and red heels. He noticed them before he noticed me; but everyone did, so I didn't mind. I'd seen his picture in the papers a few times, gone to see him in court in disguise. Well, not really a disguise, I just tried to look plain. He never noticed me, but I saw him exhibit the traits that Bobby was developing.

My God, men are so easy sometimes. Even the greatest manipulators, the incredibly smart ones like Dominic, even they are like babies looking for a tit to suck, literally: unsubtle and desperate.

That's why I kept him at arm's length for so long—close enough to keep him intrigued, but not so close that he'd get bored of me. I've slept with him twice in all the time we've known each other. That kills him, and I love it. But I'm aware how tenuous my hold over him is; he doesn't see me as his girlfriend, or a girl at all. I've read the literature, and I know that the closer we become, the quicker he'll turn and walk away.

For Bobby's sake, I can't let that happen. Not yet. Bobby had basically stopped listening to me or anyone else, and I figured the only person he might respect would be someone like himself. So, yeah, that whole heist business a while back was my idea to glue

Dom to us for a little while. The murdering side of it made me sick, but in retrospect I was an idiot for thinking they'd play nice. That Dom would play nice.

Not a mistake I'll make again.

That's a bad habit of mine, making mistakes for other people. I've only been in trouble with the law one time, a conviction for possessing crack cocaine. It was Bobby's, of course; he had a couple of baggies he was selling downtown. I'd gone to pick him up, to stop him doing it, but the cops showed up when I did—I guess they'd been doing some kind of operation out there. I took the rocks from Bobby to save him getting in more trouble. At that point he didn't have a felony conviction, and I didn't want him to have one. I failed to consider what one might do to my future, though.

Quite a lot, as it turns out. Having a felony in the job market is a little like entering the dating pool with herpes, as I explained to Dominic.

When he showed up late that night, Thursday, I knew it was over for Bobby. The way Dom was looking at me as I let him in, he had a look of curiosity on his face like all he was interested in was how I might react. Only one reason I could think of for that.

"I'm sorry," he started. "There's no way say to say this to you."

"Did the police catch Bobby?" I heard the catch in my own voice. "Or is he dead?"

"He's dead."

Dom and I stared at each for a long while. I wanted more than ever to see some flicker of life in those eyes; I wanted the mirror to crack and show me something that wasn't a reflection of my own emotions. I think that's why I didn't cry right then—I didn't want him to make some fake effort at copying me. And maybe in that moment I wanted to feel even less than he did. I sat at the kitchen table; he sat opposite me.

"What happened?" I asked eventually.

"The police found him in an abandoned house. Looks like he did it himself."

Through the fog of shock that I was trying to see through, that suggestion genuinely surprised me. "Himself? No, that doesn't sound like Bobby."

"I know."

"He was too cocky."

"I know."

"Do you . . . people like you and him. Do you even commit suicide?"

"Mostly no," he said. "But mostly we don't find ourselves in his situation."

"Meaning?"

"He killed a cop. He wouldn't feel bad about that, but he wouldn't react well to realizing he was going to be caught. To going to prison for the rest of his life."

"Is that what would've happened?" I didn't even know. "Can juveniles get life sentences?"

"We . . . the DA's office probably would've tried him as an adult. So, yes. And even if he got forty years, thirty years, that's a lifetime to a kid. I wasn't inside his head, but to begin with we don't value life the way everyone else does. Other people's, as you know, but even our own. A life in prison . . . I can see under those circumstances it making sense, yeah."

I tried not to think of little Bobby, the kid who could act sweet and kind and generous. I knew that even those moments never meant he loved me; but they did show that for a little while he wanted me to be happy. For whatever reason. I held back the tears and tried to explain why, in my heart of hearts, I knew this day would come. Or something like it.

"You know, Dom. The one thing I never wanted was to have to visit him in prison. That was always my biggest dread, seeing him get locked up. Watching the days, weeks, years go by. Watching him grow up there, and then get older and older in a jumpsuit. I don't think I could bear that."

He didn't say anything, and I knew he had no idea what to say. We didn't talk like this normally, emotionally, and I could almost hear his mind working overtime to come up with the right thing to say. The thing about Dominic, he's either scheming or blurting. Really, it's one or the other with him. He'll do both sometimes, because he knows it's also a way to mess with people. And that, I'm convinced, is his primary mission in life: to mess with people. To get them to do things for him, or just do things because he makes them. It's pretty remarkable, really, and I often wonder what would happen if he turned those abilities toward something useful, something good. That man could probably solve world hunger if he looked at it the right way. If someone told him it would really mess with some powerful people if starving Africans got fed, he could make it happen.

Yeah, I exaggerate, but after almost a year of holding him at a distance with the metaphorical version of a dog-catcher's pole, I'd seen all of him there was to see. And he didn't need to hide himself from me, which made him all the more transparent.

"I'm sorry," he said again. And there it was, Dominic at a loss for words.

He left soon after, telling me the police would be paying a visit and maybe even searching the place for evidence linking Bobby to the murder of that detective. He knew I hated the police, all authority, and took every opportunity to pass them by, ignore them. Mess with them if I had the chance. Maybe it wasn't their fault, but they'd been in my life, all my life, a nefarious presence ready to lock up my mom, my dad, my brother. I think he was suggesting that I make sure none of that evidence pointed to me, but I wasn't too sure. Either way, I had nothing to worry about on that score.

Once he'd gone, I let myself cry. To begin with, the tears were for Bobby. For a boy who'd been born with a handicap that wasn't his fault; for a boy who'd never had a chance because of that handicap; and for a boy who I'd never see alive again.

I sat on the couch and held myself, crying not just tears of sorrow but of guilt. Guilt for not being able to help him, save him. But guilt, too, because of the relief I felt. So much of my life had been devoted to quelling the fear of him, what he might do and where he might end up. Those fears were gone now, blown away by the winds that would soon blow away his ashes. That relief was palpable, and I tried not to feel too much of it.

As I sat there, clutching a tissue and dabbing at my eyes, I felt a second swell of relief rising within me. For a while now there had been another force in my life, a stressor and an unpredictability that had taken up a monumental amount of emotional and physical energy, a force I would be much happier living without. And that realization hit me hard enough to dry my tears and make me smile, a simple thought resonating loud within me.

Now that Bobby is gone, I don't need Dominic anymore.

CHAPTER THIRTEEN

DOMINIC

On Monday morning, Sergeant Brannon came by the Betts unannounced. He wore khakis, a blue blazer, and cowboy boots, and was seated outside my office when I got out of court just before eleven.

"Do you have a couple of minutes?" he asked.

"Of course, come in." I was glad McNulty was still in court.

He got up and followed me into my office. We sat down either side of my desk, and he reached into his jacket pocket and pulled out a small notebook and a tape recorder. He switched the recorder on and announced his name, my name, and the date and time.

"I know you're a busy man," he said. "I'll try not to take up too much of your time."

"No problem; I'm done with court for the day, so I'm all yours."

"Thanks. Obviously, this relates to Detective Megan Ledsome's murder."

"I figured."

"Yeah, just wrapping up a few loose ends. Just so you know where we're at, it looks like that kid, Bobby, did it and then killed himself. The gun that was beside him when you found his body, it was a match for the gun that killed Megan."

"You did the ballistics already?"

He nodded. "All hands to the pumps when a cop goes down. The ballistics guy was happy to put everything else aside for this one."

"I bet."

"Obviously that house was a shit hole, no telling who was in and out of there, but one shot to the head and no indication of a struggle. It was like he went into a little cave and took himself out."

"A shame, all of it." I shook my head sadly.

"Yeah, no doubt."

"Loose ends, you said." There was only so much fake commiserating I could pull off.

"Right, yes." He seemed to gather himself. "So Megan's husband, do you know him?"

"I don't think so."

"Greg Shindler, another cop. Good guy. So he went through some of the case papers she'd brought home, collected them all, and made a list for us."

"Ah, the second Shindler's list," I said, perhaps a little too enthusiastically.

He looked at me for a moment. "You'll excuse my lack of a sense of humor right now."

"Sorry, I wasn't trying to be glib."

He ignored the apology. "One of the things we got from Greg was a stack of letters, maybe five or six."

"The ones I told you about." *Nice work, me.*

"Yes, those. I started reading them, figured maybe there was a connection to the kid who shot her."

"Makes sense. Was there?"

"No. No mention of him at all."

I shrugged. "She said Tristan Bell is still pretty focused on bringing me down, so that doesn't surprise me."

"I'm just having a hard time getting a solid motive for this fifteen-year-old to kill a detective."

"I'm with you on that. It's beyond me that that anyone would

kill a cop. But on the other hand, I know his history and he was esca-
lating. Maybe he just escalated quicker than most."

"Nothing violent in his criminal past, though, I checked. Mostly
stealing stuff. Phones, cars, all petty crimes."

"Was he high when he did it? I've seen petty criminals do impulsive stuff, including murder, when they're high."

"No way to know; his body was found too long after."

Now, that right there was a lie, and I wondered why he told
it. Whether or not drugs were found in a body depended, in
cases like this where there was no real decomposition, on when
the person died and not on when they were found. In other
words, if they lived long enough to metabolize the drugs, then
they'd show clean at autopsy, but if they died while hopped up,
the coroner would be able to identify what they'd taken. I could
only conclude that he was hiding information from me, which
meant he was suspicious about something. If I had to guess, I'd
say it was about me.

"That's a shame," I said.

"Back to those letters. You said before you thought she wasn't
investigating you."

"Right. Why would she?"

"Just seems odd she'd keep all those letters, don't you think?"

"Not really. Maybe she had a thing for corresponding with
killers."

"Or having lunch with them." That surprised me, and he saw it.
"Sorry, I don't know why I said that, I was kidding."

"Nice that you have your sense of humor back," I said. My tone
was mild but my brain was working, wondering if this really did
mean he had something on me. But what?

"Help me out here, Dominic. I want to close the case, be sure
I've done my due diligence, but I need to find a better connection

between victim and killer. As far as I can tell, she visited him in detention one time. What kind of a connection is that?"

"For murder, not much of one, I agree." I frowned in thought. "If Detective Ledsome was looking into whatever crap Bell was peddling, wouldn't she have made notes?"

"We didn't find any, but there may be some on her computer. Greg's looking."

"I mean, I'm sure you've thought of this, of course, but she wasn't robbed? I mean, could this have been random?"

"Nothing taken. And we looked into the idea it was a gang initiation, but the kid's PO said he had no affiliation or interest in gangs."

"Maybe that changed."

"Maybe," he said. "So, you just know this kid from court."

Careful, Dom, that looks and smells like a trick question. If Ledsome knew about my "connection" with Dobby's sisters, maybe this arsehole does.

Time for a change in strategy.

"Look." I leaned forward, lacing my tone with frustration, and just a *soupçon* of anger. "I don't mean to be a dick about this, but I'm a little concerned right now. You seem to be more interested in making me look bad than anything else, and I'm not OK with that."

"Oh, no." He held up his hands in surrender. "Nothing like that, not at all."

"If Megan thought there was anything to Bell's horseshit letters, do you really think she'd meet me for lunch and tell me all about it?"

"Fair point."

"Yes, it is. I'm sorry I can't explain why this kid shot her; believe me, I'd like to. But I can't. And unless you have other questions, I need to do some work."

"Sure, of course." He stood. "Look, I didn't mean to offend you, I'm just trying to do my job."

"Honestly, I think you've already done it." I took a breath. "Sometimes a tragedy has no rhyme or reason, no matter how much we want it to."

After pocketing his recorder and notebook, he put out his hand and we shook. "That's also very true. Thanks again for your time."

He let himself out, and I watched him leave, wondering if he'd also lied about Ledsome's notes, whether they found some after all. Although it seemed to me that, even if they had, there wasn't much I could do about it now.

O

That afternoon, Brian and I had our first round of interviews for the judge position. Brian met with the four interviewers, including Judge Portnoy, from two to three, and I went in afterward.

"We're hoping to keep this pretty informal," Portnoy said when I went in. We sat at a table, Portnoy opposite me and next to Judge Tresha Barger, Brian's little friend. Two other people bookended the table. To my right sat Judge David Levingston, a jovial fellow whom I knew from criminal district court, and who always tried to talk to me about soccer. On my left was a judge I'd not met, Eric Travis. He was tall and very thin, probably in his mid-fifties, and despite being a criminal district judge, Travis seemed to wear a permanent smile on his face.

We talked about my background, and Judge Travis seemed fascinated that I was an Englishman in Texas. Not the first time I'd run into an Anglophile. "We were impressed with your idea to meet with the kids informally," he added.

"Oh, thanks," I replied. "You know, it's one of those things that seemed like a huge deal before we started doing it, but once we got going it was like, *Oh, of course we should be doing this.* Sometimes it's easy to kind of hide behind our titles, let them guide our actions instead of thinking deeply about what we're all trying to achieve here. And one of the things I like the most about being in juvenile is that we're all essentially on the same page. That's rare in the courtroom."

"Agreed," said Judge Travis. "It's very refreshing."

"Let me ask you," Portnoy said. "You're not board certified in juvenile law, are you?"

"No, I'm not."

"And you've only been here about a year?"

"That's correct."

"Do you feel that you know enough about juvenile law to be an associate judge?" she asked.

Meaning, you don't think that I do. "As I tell people, juvenile law has a steep learning curve, but it's also fairly short. I think it's also fair to say that having practiced in the district courts downtown, I have the criminal side of things nailed down pretty tightly."

"But that's just part of what a judge has to know," Portnoy pressed. For a lady who owed me a favor, she was being a little hostile.

"Of course. But ask anyone I've worked with—you have my references—I'm a fast and willing learner."

"I have one concern," Judge Barger said. "And I'm struggling with how to say it properly."

I gave her a reassuring smile. "I'm very hard to offend; please, just tell me."

"Well, I'm quite familiar with the music scene here in Austin," she said. "I know you play in a lot of the clubs, which is totally fine, of course. My worry is twofold, though. First, some of the lyrics to your songs are a little . . . racy, shall we say? I'm just not sure someone who wears a robe during the day should be singing about doing some of the things . . . you know . . ."

I do have a couple of funny songs that I sing, involving three-somes, hot tubs, and getting busted by the cops. She was really worried about this?

"Let me ask you this," I said. "If I were a writer, and I included sex or even a murder in my book, would you say that disqualifies me?"

"Well, no, I suppose not when you put it like that," she said dubiously.

"I'd like to say I'd stop singing those songs but, to be perfectly honest, one of the coolest things about this city is precisely that you *could* have a judge who also plays music and doesn't have to censor himself on stage."

"Maybe," Barger said, still unsure. "My other concern is related, I think. I do know that musicians traditionally enjoy the fruits of their labors, in terms of female admirers. Again, I worry that a judge might be putting himself in a precarious position in this regard."

Levingston cleared his throat, apparently as uncomfortable with the point she was making as I was annoyed. "I wonder," he said slowly, "if we had a female candidate here, would we be asking that kind of question? I certainly don't think I would."

Barger bristled. "I'm just trying to—"

"I know what you mean," Portnoy jumped in, hoping to right the ship. "I do think that it's reasonable to expect associate judges to comport themselves appropriately." She looked at me then, and seemed to blush, apparently remembering our shared secret. "But I think our focus should be on finding a candidate we can trust to do so, rather than try to dictate this or that." She hurried through her sentence and moved on. "Do you have any questions for us?"

I asked the ones they expected, about training, hours, and what-ever else made me sound interested. It was pretty clear to me that my first run at an associate judge position was going to fail, which was a shame because for a while now I'd really wanted the job.

DOMINIC

I am also a poor loser, to put it mildly.

Brian did his best to confirm my failure when I'd finished shaking hands with the judges and made it back to my office.

O

BRIAN

Dominic took off his tie as soon as he got into the office and threw it on his desk.

"Well, that was a waste of time," he said.

"Didn't go well?"

"Apparently being a musician isn't compatible with wearing a robe."

"Seriously? This is Austin."

"Precisely what I told them. One of the judges seemed worried I was having too much sex."

"No way!"

"Ah, well, not a problem they'll have with you, so there's that." He sank into his chair and swung his feet up onto the desk.

"They can't say stuff like that, though."

"What am I going to do about it?" Dominic said. "Sue them?"

"Good point." He seemed annoyed, and rightly. "Well, once I'm in the job, I'll put in a good word for you. Maybe that'll help."

"You're pulling on that robe mighty early."

"You just said it didn't go well for you."

"Correct, but I think you're forgetting about Mo," Dom said. "My money would be on her."

"Ah, no. I don't think so."

"Meaning?"

"Meaning I had a brief word with Judge Portnoy after my interview. Let's just say she seems to think I'm the best man, person, for the job."

"What did she say exactly?" Dom asked.

"Should I be telling you that?"

Dom closed his eyes for a second, then stared right at me. "Right, Brian. That's what's happening right now. I am asking you to tell me."

Man, he really is grumpy. "Nice try." I switched subjects, hoping he wouldn't go on about it. "I met with that detective while you were upstairs. Brannon."

Dom's head snapped up. "What did he want?"

"Just asked if I knew anything about that kid who shot his partner."

"Bannon and Ledsome were partners?"

"That's what he said. I think."

"Huh. So what did you tell him?"

"Pretty much that he was your kid and you handled his cases. I knew his face, but that's about all."

"Fair enough. He ask any questions about me?"

"A few. He talked about that whole mess you were in last year, with your roommate."

Dom chewed his lip for a moment. "I wonder why he'd mention that."

"No clue. Maybe making small talk because I didn't know the first thing about it. Basically what I read in the papers, since you don't like talking about it."

"What's done is done," he said, for like the millionth time.

"Other than that, he asked what you were like, you know, as a person and to work with."

"What did you tell him?"

"That you're an asshole, of course." I grinned so he'd know I was joking. He didn't smile back. "Nah, just, you know. Good guy, good prosecutor. Middling musician."

He must've missed that joke, too, because he sat quietly for a moment. Then he said, "I didn't know he was Megan's partner," as if that was the most important thing he'd heard all day.

CHAPTER FOURTEEN

DOMINIC

One thing about me: I don't like to lose. I think I mentioned that already.

It'd been a long time since I was in direct competition with anyone like I was with Brian for the judge job. I have to admit a certain surprise and appreciation that he'd so much as thought about playing the blackmail card. A little shortsighted, perhaps. I mean, if he really wants to work for someone who resents and despises him . . . well, given how he reacts to me, he probably won't notice.

The irony made me laugh, though: did he really have the balls to blackmail a district judge, while only doing it because he didn't have the balls to stand up to his nagging girlfriend? Idiot.

But an idiot who seemed destined to wear a robe, and most likely lord it over me.

I couldn't have that now, could I?

O

After my spell at Maidstone Hall, I'd gone on to another boarding school, Whitley College, in Hampshire. As it was far less draconian than Maidstone, I'd actually enjoyed the place, apart from the lack of girls.

At the end of my second-to-last year at the school, I'd gotten together with my buddy Johnny Hilford to carry out the Sixth Form prank of the year. The prank was one of those oddities that seems to thrive in the dusty, tradition-bound societies that are private schools. For this one someone, or several someones, from the class moving into their final year would dream up a prank that was supposed to get the whole school's attention. The trick was to strive for something that received maximum visibility, topped out in the daring stakes, but caused little permanent damage. And didn't require the police to be called.

The previous year, a couple of boys had planned ahead. At the start of the summer term, they sprinkled some mustard seeds in the shape of a penis, on the huge grassy area in the middle of first team's cricket pitch. Unnoticeable from ground level, the giant phallus was spotted from the top floor of the pavilion, and several other nearby buildings, when the cricket team turned out to play the prestigious Old Boy's match, basically an all-star team of former Whitley cricket greats. The groundsman was apoplectic; the master in charge of the school's cricket program swore vengeance on the unknown culprits; and just about every boy in the school made his way up to the pavilion to have a look, and a giggle. The prank won maximum points for attention but scored a little low on daring for my tastes. And maybe shave a few points of for a lack of class. I mean, a cock? Really?

The best ever, in most people's view, was the feathers in the school organ. It was two years previous when, on the last morning of school, everyone traipsed into Memorial Hall as we did every day for assembly. Three hundred boys and thirty or so teachers, sitting in respectful silence as the head of the music department started into the moving and powerful hymn, "Jerusalem." Within seconds, the strong notes withered in the air around us and, as we looked toward the organ to see what was wrong, feathers blasted up and out of its pipes, blue and pink plumage rising high in the air and falling like snow on every man, woman, and child in the great hall. Genius. Maximum visibility, of course, given the captive audience. Although I believe there was some permanent damage to the organ. But still, genius.

There was never any doubt in my mind that I'd be in on any prank when my turn came. My first suggestion had been to kidnap the head boy, a pompous twit who'd irritated me for years, but Johnny pointed out that the police would be called, plus everyone would know I'd done it right away. My second idea, though was gold.

At the end of every year there was a formal dinner in the cafeteria. The usual canteen slop was replaced with three courses of genuinely good food, served to us by waiters. Excitement was always high because the next day we'd be released from captivity to go home, and talk was always about our summer plans, trips, and maybe actual jobs to earn real beer money.

On the penultimate day of school, the day before this great meal, Johnny and I ate dinner together in the hexagonal, standalone cafeteria. We sat by one of the many large windows and, when no one was looking, we unlatched it, but made it look like it was still locked tight. We then moved to another table on the other side of the building and did the same thing. Plan B, you might say.

That night I lay awake in bed, willing myself not to fall asleep. Not a hard task with all the adrenaline running through me, but the hands on my watch seemed to be frozen in place. Finally midnight rolled around and I slipped out of bed, grabbed my clothes, and headed for the bathroom, rousing Johnny on the way. We dressed quickly and quietly, not saying a word. Then we crept down the main stairs to the billiard room, moving slowly in the darkness, ears pricked for any sound.

We snuck out of School House and kept close to the school buildings, staying out of the open spaces, until we got to the cafeteria. The first window we'd unlatched was still open, and we clambered in. Once inside, we took a moment to appreciate the execution of our plan thus far, secure in the knowledge that now no one would see or hear us.

Working by the light from a couple of street lamps outside, we pulled out a dozen plastic bags and went to work, filling them with every piece of silverware we could find. I wanted to go for the cooking utensils, too, but Johnny advised caution, said we wanted the food cooked still.

On a prior excursion, during the planning stages, we'd identified a nearby garden that was overgrown with bushes and high grass, so that's where we stashed the bags of silverware before creeping back into School House and making our way, undetected, into bed.

The next morning, we reaped the rewards of our derring-do. At assembly, the headmaster announced that "someone or someones unknown" had separated the school silverware from the cafeteria. It was a matter-of-fact announcement, and the headmaster made no reference to any kind of prank, though that conclusion was made obvious when he said he hoped for its return before dinnertime so that the police would not have to be called.

Johnny squirmed at the mention of the law, but that just heightened the excitement for me. Not feeling fear in a conventional way, really at all, I knew that the threat meant that a rise in the stakes and a rise in the prank's prestige, nothing more. And all day long, people were talking about nothing else, wondering who'd done it and whether the cutlery would be returned before the dinner—even whether the dinner would be canceled.

I smiled enigmatically as these questions swirled around me, and I could feel the beady eyes of the masters roaming over us, looking for signs of guilt or a reason to pull one of us aside and give us the third degree.

None of that happened. The dinner went ahead and we all ate with plastic cutlery, spoon stems and fork tines snapping left and right as the plan to serve steak forged ahead. And, naturally, conversation was less about holiday plans and all about who'd pulled off this marvelous caper. As far as I was concerned, it was utter brilliance, marred only by the fact I couldn't stand on my table and shout out that I'd done it. Unable to help myself, I dropped hints here and there, but if people pushed too hard I just remarked on the supreme conception and execution of the plan and how I *wished* I'd done it.

Our anonymity didn't last, of course. We got caught that same night. I think maybe we wanted to—what's the value of such a prank if its architects remained anonymous? Johnny and I repeated our plan in reverse, sneaking out to grab the silverware and dump it, still in bags, though the cafeteria windows. It was on our way up the broad staircase to bed that the familiar figure of our housemaster appeared, ghosting through a doorway in his robe and slippers to pin us in place with his flashlight.

Except there wasn't much he could do at that point. The next day we were all going home, so any kind of detention or forced labor was out of the question. And in truth I think he wanted to evaluate the effect of the prank before settling on a punishment, as if a part of him was a little proud that it had been executed by boys in *his* house, not one of the other four boarding houses. The following morning, he told us that because our crime had been against the whole school, we'd have to report to the headmaster at the beginning of the next term to learn our fate.

Johnny probably suffered like any empath would, worrying through his holidays about what might befall us, but of course I didn't. In any case, the following term was to be the headmaster's last at the school, too, and he was already the jolliest man on campus, even on a bad day.

Sure enough, weeks later, Johnny and I stood before him on that first day back at school, and he fixed us with an unusually serious gaze.

"I suppose you thought that was funny, did you?" he demanded.

A moment of silence, then I said, "Actually, we did, sir."

That serious look melted into a broad grin. "Well, it was! Brilliantly executed, very ingenious. No harm done, and maximum attention."

Johnny and I swapped looks. "Thank you, sir," I said, waiting for the "but."

"Buuut," he said slowly, "there needs to be a consequence, of course. So, you are both to report to the cafeteria every evening for the next two weeks to help serve your fellow students."

The import of that "consequence" soon became clear, and it was bloody marvelous: those who'd not heard we were responsible for the prank now got to hear it from us, and see the proof in us serving their puddings. Not only was this no punishment, it was like being called to the stage every night to be recognized for our prank. Whether the HM intended this or not, we sure as hell didn't care.

This reinforced a broader lesson, too, one I'd taught to myself six years earlier, and one that became increasingly significant over time. I almost always tried to curtail my impulses, limit my misdeeds to those where I could never be caught or punished. But the Great Cutlery Prank of Whitley College reminded me that sometimes, just sometimes, it's OK to go all in, to go big and trust that the winds of fate will blow kindly in your direction. You know, kind of like running away from Maidstone Hall.

It's in my nature to try to control my environment, but to do so in reckless ways. I've lived my life since that day knowing that when needs must, I might be able to pull out the big guns, so to speak, and just start blazing. Although, as the dead participants of the O.K.

Corral will attest, even a blazing gunfight could benefit from a little planning and manipulation.

This all came back to me as I pondered my situation regarding the judgeship. Like Bobby, I didn't like to be told no, and Portnoy and the other judges had basically done that. This was a problem, because the more I thought about that job the more I wanted it: an extra thirty grand a year, an office with a window (and no Brian McNulty in it), and the increased respect of my colleagues at the DA's office and the defense bar. Not to mention power. Real, actual power that I could wield at my discretion—power over the lawyers, the probation department, and the kids themselves. For people like me, power is one of the strongest aphrodisiacs life has to offer.

CHAPTER FIFTEEN

That evening, I took a table at the Crow Bar on South Congress not far from work and ordered my usual grapefruit juice and tonic. Alcohol and drugs were off-limits to me, pretty much. A man with a dangerously impulsive nature didn't need those barriers lowered further, that much I knew about myself. I did allow a little gambling now and again, the occasional bet with a friend, fellow musician, or co-worker. Nothing huge, and I always made sure the deck was stacked. I hate to lose even the smallest of wagers, like the one I had running with Bernadette at Club Steamboat the next week.

I sat there with my eyes on the door, waiting for that familiar figure, the one that could be clad in a lime-green dress or a pair of jeans or floppy pajamas, and still take my breath away.

She got there just after six, gliding through the door in black skinny jeans and a white shirt, along with a large pair of sunglasses. Heads swiveled to watch as she crossed the room and settled opposite me.

"Before I forget," she began. "Can you find out when my aunt gets out? It's soon and I need to have the room ready."

"You're too good to her." She was. It was her mother's sister, a deadbeat who was in and out of the county lockup for theft, possessing crack, public intoxication, all the stuff that deadbeats do. Blood relative or not, I'd have dumped that crone years ago.

"I know." She gave me a half smile. "But one day she'll win the lottery, and then I'll murder her for the proceeds."

"Good plan. I'll find out tomorrow; I think I can ask the deputy at work to look up the date."

"Thanks. So, Sergeant Brannon came to see me today."

Small talk over, I guess. "He's been busy. Buy you a drink?"

"Water's fine. How so, busy?"

"He paid a visit to me and McNulty, too."

"I'm sure he's just doing his job," she said. "Right?"

"Sure. Anything of interest come up?"

"He asked about you," she said, "which makes me think we shouldn't see each other for a while." She looked pale, sad, but even so I longed to kiss those lips, cherry red even without makeup. "I hear that the police are known to follow the subjects of their inquiries."

"Maybe. What did he ask about me and what did you say?"

"Whether I knew you. I told him that I knew you as Bobby's prosecutor, that you seemed fair, but that we'd never done more than swapped hellos in court."

So she lied. That could be dangerous. "You get the impression he thinks otherwise?"

She shrugged, and when the waiter came to the table I asked for two glasses of water. "No clue," she said.

"He may be looking into the heist. He's definitely interested in the letters Bell's sending to Ledsome, and why she talked to Bobby in detention."

"Lucky for me, I don't know anything about any of that," she said.

I winked. "Yeah, me neither."

"He asked if we knew Ledsome, too. If I knew her."

"I'm assuming you didn't."

"Right. I told him that I'd never even seen her, let alone met her. And that as far as I knew, outside of the detention visit, Bobby didn't know her from Eve, either."

"He's thorough," I said. "I'll give him that."

"Yeah, he was asking me about some of the things I've been

thinking about," she said. "Like, why would a fifteen-year-old kill a cop? And why, specifically, would Bobby do it?"

"Well, we both know the answer to that, at least potential answers. Not exactly things we can lay out for Brannon, though."

Her head tilted downward. "I guess that's true."

"It is. So did you tell him you think Bobby *didn't* kill her? Play the grieving sister?" I realized the moment I said it that it'd come out wrong. I figured she knew me well enough to know why, to cut me some slack, but I was mistaken. She took her sunglasses off and looked me in the eye, then shook her head slowly and stood.

"Playing?" she repeated, her voice as cold and hard as ice. "Something tells me that I'm the only one around here not playing at something. Like I said before, I think it would be better if we don't see each other for the foreseeable future. Now, if you'll excuse me, I have a funeral to plan."

She walked out on me then, with no change to the natural and mesmerizing sway of her hips, no change to the proud straightness of her spine. She left the way she came in, in total charge of everyone in the room, including me.

○

On Tuesday morning I brought an extra latte to the deputy in charge of courthouse security at the Betts, Mike Trejo. He was a good-looking guy, bald with expressive brown eyes that could look mean as hell but were usually laughing. He was a boxer in his spare time, and coached his kids' flag football team. Stand-up guy, and always willing to help out us prosecutors.

"You need a favor," he said with a grin as he accepted the latte.

"A wee one, yes." I nodded and attempted to look sheepish.

"Tell me."

"I was just curious about something, but if you can't do it, or shouldn't, then just let me know. Not a big deal."

"Nah, man, tell me," he said again.

I sighed. "It's just . . . weird. I just feel like someone's been following me for a couple of weeks."

His eyes widened. "You serious?"

"Yeah. I mean, I'm sure it's my imagination, but I keep seeing the same car and the same guy—but every time I look his way, he takes off. Not in a panicked way, he just . . . you know."

"Dude, that is weird. You want me to make a report?" He pointed to his computer on the table where he spent most of his day, next to the screening machine and with a view of the parking lot. "I can do it right now."

"No, I don't think so. It's probably just PTSD after almost being framed by that tool Bell. Paranoia, whatever you want to call it," I said, miming embarrassment.

"I don't know, Dom, I mean you're a prosecutor. You gotta have pissed off a lot of people, no?"

"Maybe. I try to be fair, though. And I always imagine that people, defendants included, realize I'm just doing my job; it's never personal."

"Not for you, but for some criminal going to prison . . . Seriously, you should at least make a report."

"Let me see if I can get a license plate first, or maybe a picture of the guy. I really don't want to jump to conclusions."

"If you're sure. What do you need from me?"

"I was just going to ask you to keep an eye out. We're all kind of sitting ducks, walking in from the parking lot."

"Sure, of course. I'll tell the other deputies, too."

"Thanks, Mike. Oh, I was also wondering, do you have access to the same info the deputies do at the jail?"

"Yeah, it's all on the computer system."

"Great," I said. "So you can look up release dates, which unit inmates are in, all that good stuff?"

"All of it," he said. "I can tell you if they've had discipline issues, who their cellmates are, if they have dietary restrictions."

"Perfect. And you won't get in trouble for looking someone up for me, kind of a favor."

"No, man, we're good. They don't keep track of that; and, even if they did, I don't know anyone who'd mind." He pulled out a pen and a small notepad from his top pocket. "What do you need?"

"I can't believe it's that simple."

"It's a new age, Dom." He grinned. "Everything's computerized, so it really is simple. I'll print out what I find, bring it to you."

I gave him the information, and he left his post at the entrance, nodding at his two colleagues to take over, then went into his small office down the hallway that led to the main courtroom. *Sometimes things are that easy*, I thought, and went back to my office.

Ten minutes later, Mike knocked on the door and waved a single piece of paper at me. "Just four cellmates; he wasn't there long. Need anything else?"

"No, but thanks, I appreciate it."

"You can just go online to the county website to see if any of them are still locked up, if that's what you need."

"Yeah, we use that inmate locator a lot," I said. "You'd be surprised how often our witnesses don't show up to court or meetings because they've been locked up on a warrant, or for beating their spouse."

"Nah, man, I wouldn't be surprised in the least." He gave me a parting wave. "Keep your eyes peeled and holler if you need anything else."

What I needed was for Sergeant Jeremy Brannon to leave me and my lady alone. To close the case on Bobby and go about finding all the other bad guys rattling around my growing city. What I needed, and planned to make sure I got, was a dramatic, all-out display that I was the victim in that case, then and now.

But first things first. At lunch I bought myself a brand-new computer, small enough to fit in my already-full bag, and cheap enough that I could pay for it in cash. I sat in the break room and ran searches on the four names that Trejo had given me. First up, Ricardo Sotolongo. According to the Travis County website, he was still locked up in Del Valle, so he wasn't a candidate. Next up was Travis Lee White, who had apparently been released. Duly noted. A Web search didn't come up with any news stories or other information about Mr. White, so I put him aside for the moment.

The third name was Jose Gutierrez. I typed that into the search box, and it gave me three hits, one of whom matched the date of birth on Trejo's printout. Still locked up. Or locked up again, judging from the recent booking date.

The fourth name was John Eastcott, a gentleman who had been released from Del Valle Correctional Facility some months ago, in a body bag. According to the *Statesman*, some unpleasantness had arisen among a few inmates, and Mr. Eastcott had been taken to task for his racially insensitive views. Taken to task by three fellow inmates bearing shivs.

Which left just me and Travis Lee White. I had no idea who he was or what he'd done to wind up in a cell with Tristan Bell, but if, sometime down the road, the police investigated him for stalking me, I'd like to find out a little about him on my own.

Well, maybe with some help from my good friend Brian.

CHAPTER SIXTEEN

I slapped the desk in frustration, making McNulty jump. "Jeez, Dom, you'll give me a heart attack," he said.

If that's all it takes, I thought, but said, "Sorry, old chap, I swear my Versadex account is jinxed. It's like every fifth report I try to run gets jammed up. Very frustrating."

"You're the computer whiz around here, so don't ask me to fix it."

"I'm wondering whether it's a hardware or software problem."

"No clue. Want me to run something for you?"

"Yeah, please. Wait, no. Mind if we try something?"

He tore his eyes away from his Facebook feed and looked over at me. "Try something?"

"Yeah. I log into Versadex using your username and password but on my computer. Then I try and run a report. If it works, then I know it's my account that's screwed. It if doesn't work, then it's the computer somehow."

"I guess," he said.

"Right? Makes sense to me."

"Except, I can't give you my info to log in. Remember? We signed that user agreement with Austin PD saying we'd keep it confidential."

"I don't think they meant from each other," I said, as patronizingly as I could.

"Well, I'm pretty sure so. They like to keep a record of everyone who logs in, what they look at. You know, store that info."

"So?"

"So," he said, as if I were the dolt, "if we're all using each other's accounts, that information would be incorrect. Useless."

"Fine." I sighed and stood up. "If you really think so. You can log in, I won't look." I made a show of moving away from my desk and turning my back to him as he went over to my keyboard.

"There," he said a moment later. "I'm in. what do you need?"

"Let's just see if it works. Go to your history and print the last report you pulled up. The last short one;—we don't need to be destroying trees for this little experiment."

I turned and saw the offense report appear on my screen. "Works fine," he said. "Does that mean it's your account that's corrupted somehow?"

"I think so. I'll put in a work order for them to look at it."

"Can I log out of here now?"

"Yes, thank you." I gave him a grin. "And no user agreements violated; what good little prosecutors we are."

"I am," he said. "They can thank me." Then he got off his high horse and added, "After all, prospective judges can't be swapping passwords and pissing off the cops, eh?"

"Very true, I really shouldn't be."

He snorted on his way back to his desk. "Good one, Dom. If you're lucky, it'll be your turn next time."

"Right. I forgot." I waited until he'd turned back to his social media before picking my phone up from the stack of law books beside my computer. I stopped the video recording, turned the volume all the way down, and replayed the last two minutes. Brian's fat fingers stabbed at the keyboard, fast enough that I missed his username and password the first time around, but slow enough that I got them on the second showing.

As much as I wanted to do it right there and then, I knew I had to wait until he left the office. If Versadex somehow showed two

Brian McNultys logged in at the same time, well, that might raise a suspicion or two. The clocked ticked slowly past the three o'clock hour, and then slowed until it hit four. Brian didn't notice for ten more minutes.

"Right," he said finally. "That about all the justice I can dispense for one day."

"The world's a better place. Nice work."

He gathered his *Doctor Who* lunchbox and his computer bag, then gave me a thumbs-up as he left, saying, "See ya for more of the same tomorrow, mate."

"You bet," I said, through gritted teeth. "Mate."

I made sure he was gone and didn't come back, like for his *Teletubbies* water bottle or whatever. Then I logged on as Brian McNulty and put Travis Lee White's name and date of birth into Versadex.

And if I'd believed in God, I would've thanked him.

Travis White was a loser. Not in the dorky, annoying way that Brian was a loser, but in the way that life had kicked him in the balls and he'd crumpled, lying in a heap on the ground and unable to get up as everyone in sight put the boot in, making sure that he never truly recovered.

Twenty-seven contacts with Austin police in the last five years, some as a victim, a couple as a witness, and nineteen as the suspect. You name it, he'd done it. Possessing marijuana, trespassing on private property, shoplifting, assault. It was a gently arcing, one-man crime wave, and the beauty of it was that it showed a slight but unmistakable escalation. From property crime to misdemeanor assault, to felony evading in a motor vehicle, then unlawful carrying a firearm, followed by robbery, his latest.

I studied his mug shot. A stocky man with pale skin and tattoos up his neck, jail tattoos of such shitty quality that I couldn't read them. He had a buzz cut and a goatee that was way too long, a scraggly, wiry waterfall disappearing down and out of the picture. His eyes looked black and disinterested, and I wondered about him. They say that 25 percent of inmates are psychopaths, as opposed to about 1 percent of the regular population, but I'd not much cared until now. Even if he was, most of them were idiots, and, given the number of times he'd been caught and jailed, any lack of soul was likely to be matched by a lack of wits.

The most recent address for him was an apartment complex close to downtown, one I'd heard of: Meadowbrook Apartments. Again, no meadows or brooks to be found there, just poor families, criminals, and kids throwing rocks at each other. Cops called it "Murderbrook" for all the gang activity and warrants they served on the place. Ironically, the entire neighborhood around it was bristling with gentrification, fancy homes crammed into small lots, such that the nearby elementary school was half filled with kids delivered in Land Rovers and Teslas, while the other half were walked down South Fifth Street by parents in flip-flops and pajamas.

Of all the projects in Austin, then, it wasn't the worst to live in, and I thought I knew where to start learning a little more about my subject. I phoned the management office at Meadowbrook and put on my most official voice, toning down the accent because it sometimes threw people a little, when I asked after Travis White. The woman on the other end hesitated.

"Travis County DA's office, you said?"

"Yes, ma'am."

"And your name again?"

"Brian. Brian McNulty," I lied. For no particular reason, and I instantly wished I hadn't.

"You know, I don't think I can give that information out over the phone. If you had a warrant or something . . ."

I knew she was unsure and just throwing out words she'd heard on *Law & Order*, but I stayed friendly. "Oh, I'm not looking to search his place or anything like that, just confirm he lives there, and which apartment."

"I don't think I can. Can you tell me why?"

"Not really," I said. "State secret." *I know irrelevant buzzwords, too.*

"Oh. Well, sorry."

"Hmm. How about this. I won't ask for any specific information, but if he lives in the complex, maybe you don't hang up. If he doesn't live there anymore, you hang up straight away."

"Oh, I guess . . ." Silence came down the line for a good ten seconds.

"Well," I said. "Thank you so much for your cooperation, and your professional discretion, I appreciate it very much. One last thing. Do you guys have security cameras on the premises?"

"No. We used to, but people would either vandalize them or steal and resell them, so we stopped replacing them. None left."

"That's a shame. I'm seeing a lot of crime in that area. What about security guards?"

"Only until two in the morning, starting again at six."

"Good to know. Thanks again for the help."

So he still lived there. The police report I'd read didn't give a specific apartment number, so I thought for a moment, then grabbed my keys and went out to my car.

I turned right on South Congress, then left on Oltorf to South Fifth to Mr. White's closest library. The Twin Oaks Library was classic Austin. Its books represented Austin's artistic community, of course, but the building itself was also typical of the city: the exterior was made of recycled bricks, while the inside featured recyclable carpeting and furniture fabrics and had a sophisticated lighting system that automatically dimmed when there was sufficient daylight.

At the circulation desk, I showed my badge and official Travis County ID. I also flashed my brightest smile at the prettier of the two girls working there.

"Hi, I'm from the Travis County District Attorney's Office; I wonder if you can help me?"

Her eyes lit up. "Sure, what do you need?"

I gave her a conspiratorial wink and lowered my voice. "It's a little sensitive." I looked around at the many patrons milling around. "Can we talk over here?"

Without waiting for an answer, I moved to the reference section, which was empty except for an older man wearing gigantic earphones.

Her name tag said Rose, and she was a cute little thing with ponytails and no makeup. She had tattoos on her arms, brown ones drawn in henna.

"What is it?" she asked, a little wide-eyed.

"So we have this new program, kind of a community-outreach thing. We're trying to move away from the traditional model of criminal justice and rehabilitation. You know, good guys versus bad guys and as much prison time as possible. Totally outdated," I said. "And utterly ineffective."

She clasped her hands together. "Oh, my God. I'm so glad to hear you say that. The prison industrial complex is a moneymaker for private enterprise. It's cashing in on the misery of those who need the most help."

Whatever. "Yes! I totally agree. More to the point, my boss agrees. Anyway, I'm supposed to help a particular gentlemen who, just between us, has been through the wringer. I've been here a few times to meet him, I don't know if you've noticed."

She seemed caught out, uncertainty in her eyes. "Err, no, I don't think . . . I must not have been here."

I gave her a lingering look. "Oh, you were here, I noticed you all right."

She blushed, and may even have peed herself, I wasn't sure. "Oh, I'm sorry. I can't believe—"

"Oh, it's OK. The thing is, my guy, the one I'm supposed to help, didn't show up either time. I didn't want to ask publicly, you know, make it obvious that he's a . . . you know." *A worthless criminal.*

"Right, no, of course," she gushed. "Wow, that's so sensitive of you." She frowned. "I don't know how to help, unless you feel like you can tell me his name, maybe what he looks like?"

"Well," I hesitated. "I guess I can do that. I mean, if you saw us together now you'd know, and we're both county employees, right? It's not like you'd ever say anything to him about this."

"Oh, God, no, never," she reassured me hurriedly.

"I know, for sure. So, his name is Travis." I pulled a piece of paper from my jacket pocket and showed her his mug shot. "Travis White," I said. "Do you recognize him?"

The chances were good. As much as local authorities liked to hack away at library budgets, they remained lifesavers for the dregs of society. They provided books for those who could, and wanted to, read; but, more importantly, they provided for free the kinds of resources that a lot of poor people couldn't afford. Most notably, the Internet. Also, I knew that this library provided job assistance, including résumé writing and online applications at nearby businesses, mostly restaurants and big-box stores like Wal-Mart.

And, according to the library's website, the delightful Rose McCracken upon whom I was shamelessly pouring the charm, happened to be one of the three librarians designated the task of overseeing these resources.

"Yes!" she exclaimed, then shushed herself. "Sorry, but yes. He usually comes in around six. Not every day, but most."

"Oh, great." I checked my watch. "Maybe I'll come back. Does he have a car, or walk?"

"He has an older car," she said. "Red, a Honda I think."

"And you close at nine?"

"Yes. You want me to tell him you were here, that you're coming back?"

"No, if you do that he'll know you know . . . I don't think we want to risk embarrassing the guy."

"Oh, right, sorry." She rolled her eyes at herself. "I can't believe I suggested that."

"No," I said. "You've been so helpful, I really appreciate it."

"Oh, you know what? He comes to an AA meeting here on Wednesday nights. Seven o'clock in the large conference room."

I gave her another warm smile, and her mouth opened as if she wanted to say or ask something, but she didn't. I squeezed her arm warmly and walked out of the library to my car.

CHAPTER SEVENTEEN

The next morning I was in court, tucked behind my prosecutor's table as another slew of unrepentant kids shuffled in front of Judge Portnoy. She normally handled only the serious cases, but every now and again she presided over a docket of regular cases, the marijuana-possession and shoplifting tripe I saw every day.

At eleven she adjourned for a break, inclining her head for me to meet her in the judge's hallway that runs behind the courts. I sidled out there as surreptitiously as I could, with a good idea of what she wanted: either help or information.

Once I'd discovered that there was no official report of her little indiscretion, I'd gone back and told her. I didn't say anything about my phone call with Chipelo, but I did mention who'd been sitting in the car, watching the whole thing unfurl. As a result, she knew what McNulty's game was and probably wanted more advice on how to stop him. Or, at the least, to make sure there were no more copies floating about. As for me, I was curious about whether he'd had the balls to actually make an explicit demand or two yet.

"Let's go to my office," she said.

I followed her down the hall and she held the door to her office, closing it firmly behind me.

"Can I assume he made his play?" I asked.

"Yes and no. He hasn't said anything directly, I think he's smart enough to know that if I do decide to go to the police, without any kind of threat or demand, there's no blackmail case."

"Smart? That doesn't sound like McNulty."

She clenched her jaw, unamused. "I was hoping you might have a suggestion or two for me."

"He's not said anything at all?"

"He walked into that interview like it was a done deal. The way he looked at me . . . he knew I'd seen it. That it was him."

"Well, yes," I said. "Of course. But what happens when he gets that robe?" *The one I now want so badly.* "Maybe you should call his bluff. He'd be utterly ruined if you stood up to him."

"The problem is, so would I," Portnoy said. "And I have a damn site more to be ruined than he does."

"Do you really want to work with him, though? I mean what's that going to be like?"

"I have two more years, and then I can retire," she said. "Two more years, and then I don't care what he or anyone else does because I'll be on a beach in Aruba downing margaritas. But until then, I need my job and reputation intact."

"He's not said a word to me," I told her. "But he sure is cocky about getting that job."

"Yeah, well." Her tone was resigned. "I guess he should be."

"What if the others on the panel don't like him?"

"They'll defer to me. This is my territory, so to speak."

"Then I guess just go along with him and hope he doesn't screw you over once it's a done deal."

"I was thinking, I could maybe meet with him and record it. Get him to say something incriminating. Then either confront him and make him give up any copies, or even go to the police with it and have them pressure him. Without prosecuting, though."

"Both of those assume he'll incriminate himself. I know I don't think highly of his intelligence, but surely he's not that dumb." I shook my head. "Also, if you go to the police, it's going to get out. No matter what they promise, it'll leak out. This is Internet gold."

"To you maybe," she snapped.

"Just telling you like it is. Trying to help."

"Yes, sorry." She didn't sound it, though. "Well, we should get back to court. Will you let me know if he says anything to you?"

"Of course, absolutely."

After lunch, Brian was nowhere to be seen, but at three he appeared and clattered about with his lunchbox and briefcase. Once he finally settled in he turned to me, too quickly for me to put in my earbuds and crank some Kings of Leon.

"Hey," he said. "What's the scoop on the poker game?"

"Why, you chickening out?"

"Heck no. Got my stash of cash ready to go."

"Good, hang onto it. Game's been pushed back; it's in two weeks," I said. "A couple of the chaps had family trouble. You know how it is with those married guys, always needing permission to go out."

"Yeah, that's not me."

"I bet. Cindy not wanting to tie the knot?"

"It's Connie. And she hasn't said anything. Why buy the milk when you can get it for free, eh?"

"I'm sure she'd love the cow comparison."

"Yeah, well, you know what I mean."

"Hey, you want to go to the range today? I feel like shooting something."

O

BRIAN

Dominic probably guessed this about me, but I actually do have to run things by Connie. That's why I was asking about the game, so I could give her plenty of notice. Not that she's possessive or anything, or particularly controlling, she just isn't a great one for spontaneity. Especially mine.

Which is why his sudden invitation to the shooting range had made me hesitate. But, then again, I sure did want to shoot with Dominic. I made a snap decision.

"Yeah, cool. What time?"

"You usually knock off around four. If you can bear to wait an extra thirty minutes, we can head over to APD's range."

"They let us use that?"

"They let me use it. I had a case with one of the instructors, he was assaulted while on patrol. Some baby-momma racked him in the face with a box of baby wipes, believe it or not."

I laughed. Dominic has the best stories. "For real?"

"Yeah, she wouldn't take my plea offer, so we went to trial and the jury hammered her."

"How long?"

"Nine years."

"Holy shit!"

"Yeah, it was hilarious."

"Yeah?" Nine years seemed like a long time for just that, and certainly not hilarious.

"Yep. I got to make all kinds of puns. Like how, after she hit him, she tried to make a clean getaway. How her lawyer was trying to wipe away the seriousness of assaulting a cop. Some others, I forget. Anyway, the cop appreciated the humor and the sentence, so once the range closes to cadets for the day, he lets me shoot there."

"That's way cool, I'm in." I took out my phone, then saw the look on Dom's face. "I'm gonna *tell* Connie, not ask her."

Lucky for me she didn't pick up, so I left a message that I'd be home around six thirty.

"You have your gun on you?" Dom asked when I was done.

"I keep it in the car. I still don't have a concealed-carry license."

"Ammo?"

"Loads, actually. I keep meaning to go to Red's and shoot." *But Connie doesn't approve, so I don't.*

I followed him out to the APD range at the academy in southeast Austin, having never been there before. He introduced me to Lieutenant Brett Bailey, the firearms instructor. I wanted to make a joke about the baby wipes case, but nothing came to mind so I just shook his hand and thanked him for letting me use the place.

"Hey, any friend of Dominic's is a friend of mine."

We stopped at the entrance to the range proper and helped ourselves to earphones and protective glasses, then walked through heavy doors into a hangar-like space with a concrete floor and a low ceiling that was covered in some kind of sound- or bulletproof material. Probably both. Lieutenant Bailey had already put up two targets, clipped to a wooden bar at the back of the range, upperbody outlines of a bad guy with a gun. Bailey gave us a wave and left us alone.

I was suddenly nervous; I'd not fired my gun in over a year and wasn't very good then. Knowing Dom, he'd be an excellent shot and make fun of me if I wasn't.

"Fifteen yards to start?" Dom asked.

"Sure," I said.

"You got fourteen in that magazine?"

"I think so. Same as yours, right?"

He took my gun, looked at it quickly, then released the magazine and counted the bullets inside. "Yep, same. Let's do seven at the head, then see if we can hit the gun."

"I thought cops always went for body shots."

"We're not cops."

I waited for him to shoot first, the gun heavy in my hand and getting heavier as I waited. When it came, the explosion from his gun seemed to be amplified by the earphones, not muffled, I'd forgotten how loud guns were. But when my turn came I squeezed the trigger, aiming generally for the head. I counted off seven shots, and Dominic's presence disappeared with my concentration. After those seven, I lowered the sight toward the black outline of the bad guy's gun before squeezing the trigger seven more times.

When we were done, we holstered our guns and I realized how sweaty my palms were.

"All clear?" he asked.

I wasn't sure what he meant, but nodded. "All good."

He gestured for me to follow him up to the targets, but I could already see how I'd done. Dominic took a quick look at his and then stood in front of mine. "Two in the head, and you knocked the gun out of his hand twice," he said. "Not bad."

"And you?"

"Seven and five." He pointed to a cluster of my shots that had hit the bad guy's neck. "See this? I think you're overcompensating for the kick of the gun. I always used to until Brett explained what was happening. You don't realize you're doing it, but you're pushing the tip of the gun down in preparation for the kick. Hence the low shots."

"You think?"

"Yeah. And if you're doing that, you're probably gripping the gun too hard. Are your hands all sweaty?"

"Definitely."

"Vicious cycle. You grip the gun too hard and your hands get sweaty, so you're afraid of losing control and grip tighter." He nudged me with a friendly elbow. "Rookie mistake."

"I guess."

"Let's go again. Just focus on the sight at the end of the barrel, not the close one. Same as last time?"

"OK, sure." We went back to our positions and took a moment to reload. Well, he took a moment, I took a few more, the bullets were slippery in my fingers and I found the spring in the magazine hard to push against.

"All right," he said, when I was done. "Ready? Then the range is hot. Fire when you're ready."

The shots seemed quieter this time, and I focused on relaxing my grip and keeping the front sight on the target. I hit the head four times and the gun three.

We shot from twenty yards, then twenty-five, my aim improving with repetition then worsening as we moved back. It was fun, though, and by the time we wrapped up an hour had gone by.

"We need to clean up?" I asked.

"Yeah, they have this cool device that collects shells. I'll get that and you grab our targets; we need to put them in the stack at the front."

I unclipped the now-shredded targets and walked them over to a pile on a table by the main doors, then watched as Dominic ran what looked like a push lawnmower over the places we'd been standing, collecting the shell casings. When he was done, he showed me how to strip down my gun and clean it, using the long table at the front of the range.

"An Englishman shouldn't be showing a Texan how to shoot and clean a gun," I joked.

He grunted. "No worries. Now you know, eh?"

"You may need to show me this bit again." The gun mechanism looked a little complicated, which bit went where, exactly. "But hopefully I've got the actual shooting down a little better. Appreciate the tips—that was fun."

"Welcome." He checked his watch. "Hey, I gotta run. You can find your way home?"

"GPS is my friend."

He nodded and left me there, trying to slide the barrel back into place. I finally managed it, then turned to look back at the empty range. Connie would be upset at the short notice, but I'd just shot guns with Dominic at the Austin Police Academy's gun range. She could deal. And I didn't even care that he might be doing this to suck up to a potential judge, not one bit. I was having fun.

CHAPTER EIGHTEEN

DOMINIC

My gun went into the glove compartment, and I made the trip back to the Twin Oaks Library, parking across the street instead of using the lot in case the place had erected eco-friendly, recyclable surveillance cameras. I sat and watched.

A few minutes before seven, he arrived in a clapped-out Honda Civic from the mid '90s. He parked in a handicapped spot, and that got my juices flowing. Here was an ex-con looking to improve his life, parking illegally. Not that I needed a reason to dislike him for what I was planning; the greatest benefit of having no empathy was that I never needed to make excuses to myself for the way I treated people. But I did like to imagine myself as a generally decent guy, so it never hurt if I could manufacture a reason that some dolt brought harm upon himself, and an ex-con taking up a handicapped space out of laziness or entitlement fit just fine.

I waited for the meeting to end, resisting the temptation to break into his car there and then. At eight fifteen he wandered out of the library, ignoring the inquiring looks of a young couple who had also noticed his parking spot on their way in to return armfuls of books. I tucked in behind his car as he made the short trip back to Meadowbrook, not even a mile. That annoyed me even more. Lazy slob should have walked.

Once I knew which apartment was his, I called it a night. Two objectives achieved was plenty. But I did sit in my car outside my place, wondering if I'd made it too complicated, if I was pushing my luck.

But that's another problem I have. Pushing my luck is a way to feel things. You see, when you have an absence of fear, an inability to love, and a total lack of empathy, there's a hole inside that you're always aware of, that you're always looking to fill. Feeling things is important; it's why people read books, listen to music, and watch romantic comedies. Music cracks the mirror for me, but mostly when I'm behind the guitar; and, while I appreciate the elegance of a well-turned sentence, I still don't feel anything much when I read a book.

Filling that hole takes a little more. And sometimes I push myself too hard, too far, and take risks that I don't immediately recognize as dangerous. But I also fill that hole with logic, in the sense that I try to plan my thrills so that it's only other people who get hurt. And, yes, I'm well aware of how that sounds.

After a little analysis, a balancing of the odds, I decided that not only was I too far in to make any changes, but that I was having too much fun. I thought back to the Great Cutlery Prank and reassured myself that despite all that I'd been through and all that I'd done, fate and the gods were on my side. The only nagging worry I had as I let myself into my apartment was that I didn't believe in fate or any gods.

I decided to take a nap in my clothes, setting my alarm for three that morning, and when it went off, I was already dressed in black jeans and a black, long-sleeved shirt. I drove back to Meadowbrook, careful not to speed or run lights, and signaling at every turn. When I got there, I drove through the entire apartment complex twice, watching for security guards and cameras, just in case my contact had been mistaken or lying.

Travis White's car was parked between a motorcycle and an

ancient brown truck, sitting deep in a patch of darkness. A tall wooden pole stood close by, but someone had broken the two lights atop it, and I silently thanked them.

In Bobby's short life I'd done much to help him, to guide and teach him. But he'd taught me a few things, too, and one of them was how to break into a car. I'd looked online—you can learn anything there—but with his guidance and some practice at the mall parking lot, I'd gotten almost as good as he was. And a 1990s Honda Civic was a doddle. Within five seconds I had the front door open, nothing broken or even scratched. I checked to make sure his glove compartment was filled with the usual array of papers and trash, and added my own little gift. Then I popped the trunk and checked his spare tire, sprinkling gift number two around it but out of sight.

I was in and out of that squalid little patch of asphalt and sub-human housing in less than ten minutes, at home and in bed before four a.m. Which gave me a few hours of sleep before I had to get up and make my acquaintance with Travis Lee White in the flesh.

O

I've never known a con or ex-con to be an early riser. Maybe it's in the genes. Or maybe they become criminals because they're too lazy to work for a living, so of course they sleep late. Whatever the reason, I wasn't wrong about him.

White made his appearance in the parking lot at ten a.m. on Thursday morning, an hour after I'd gotten there. I stood behind a tree about forty yards away and watched him walk to his car. When he got to it, he stopped and stood there with his hands on his hips, shaking his head with annoyance. I'd parked right beside him where the motorcycle had been, and I mean *right* beside. No way he could get in on the driver's side, but he stayed there for a moment, wondering if he could and looking around for the dumbass who'd blocked him out.

Eventually he came to the conclusion that he'd have to get in through the passenger door and climb across. Apparently he'd not been doing his yoga, because it was an almost comical struggle and, of course, it being a tiny car didn't help. At first he sat in the passenger seat and tried to swing his legs over to the driver's side. But he was too big or inflexible and couldn't manage it that way. Then he shifted his upper body to the driver's side, and tried to bring his legs over, but that was a fail, too.

The winning formula was to kneel on the passenger seat, facing backward, then shift over to the driver's side, still facing the rear of the car. Then all he had to do was corkscrew his body around and drop into the seat. By that time, two things had happened: first, he'd worked himself into a righteous anger, his face red and his fists thumping the steering wheel. Second, I'd let myself into my car and was watching him with an amused expression on my face. For a moment he didn't realize I was there, but as soon as he did, his eyes bulged and his mouth fell open. He wound his window down.

"What the fu—" he started to yell.

I just gave him a cheery wave through my closed window and shouted, "Have a nice day!"

I eased forward and saw him fumbling with his keys, no doubt stabbing at the ignition to dash after me, but by the time his ancient wreck of a vehicle had cranked to life, he was a little red dot in my mirror. I didn't speed away from him, though, instead I pulled into the library parking lot, pretty sure he'd head that way. I tucked my car behind a van so that I couldn't be seen by anyone until they actually passed me.

Sure enough, Travis White puttered by and I could swear he was still crimson with rage. I sure hoped so. I let him get a hundred yards ahead, then I pulled out of my spot and started to follow him. He drove north along Fifth Street, all the way to Barton Springs Road, where he turned right. I was having to make this up as I went along, this wee part of the plan, but it was to my advantage that he was heading roughly in the direction of Gardner Betts.

I had to make educated guesses at this point, which was not a big deal because it wouldn't matter if they didn't pan out. If my plan wasn't executed this morning, it could happen this afternoon, tomorrow, or even the next day. He had no idea I was behind him, the oblivious idiot, and I followed him all the way to the Chevron on Riverside and South Congress. He turned in, and ten seconds later I did, too, taking the only available pump. He'd pulled into an empty parking spot in front of the gas station's store, Riverside Grocery, but still hadn't spotted me. I had to be careful from now on, play it just right, because this place would have cameras, and in a day or two a policeman would come asking for the footage of what was about to happen.

Even though I didn't really need gas, I slid my credit card through the reader and put the nozzle in my tank. I turned my back on White as he went into the store, and I watched the numbers on the pump speed by. The tank filled up quickly, clanking to a stop while Travis White was still inside. I reholstered the nozzle and locked my car, heading for the store. Once inside, I lingered behind the shelves of chips and crackers, my head down but White always in view. He was buying beer, of course, a twelve-pack of Miller Light, and several bags of chips.

As he made for the exit, I grabbed a bottle of Diet Coke from one of the glass-fronted fridges, dropped two dollars on the counter, and stepped to the door just as it was closing.

Walking slowly, I put a car between White and me and waited until he was half in and half out of his Civic before I said anything.

"Hey, fuckface," I said, slowly and clearly, but without looking at him. "Learn how to park next time."

His arms were full of snack food, and he fell into his seat and looked up at me, his eyes wide with surprise. I could see the wheels turning, the recognition rising like the morning sun to ignite his wrath all over again.

"It's you," was all he could manage to say, though.

"Yeah, dumbass." I started moving toward my car. "It's me. And it was fun watching you pretzel yourself; we should do it again sometime."

He threw his recent purchases onto the passenger seat as I jogged to my car, jumped in, and squealed out of there. He didn't get his crap box started in time to follow me, at least according to my rearview mirror, but I jinked down a couple of side streets on my way to Gardner Betts just to be sure.

When I pulled into the parking lot in front of the Betts, I made a good show of staying in my car and looking all around, my head on a swivel when I finally got out. Once I was inside the building, Trejo nodded and said, "You OK, Dom? You're late and were acting weird out there." He nodded toward the large glass windows that overlooked the parking lot.

"Remember what I said about being followed?"

"Yeah, you see him again?"

"Did I ever. I got gas at the Chevron down there." I jerked my thumb in the vague direction of the Riverside Chevron. "I'd seen this little red Honda behind me, that car I mentioned the other day." He nodded along, as if I'd mentioned the make and color before. "Well, he pulled in but didn't go to any of the pumps. Anyway, I basically confronted him, asked why he was following me."

"Shit, you did?"

"Yeah. He said, 'Fuck you, you'll get yours.' So I said, 'What the hell does that mean?' Then he reached over to the passenger side and said something like, 'How about you get it right here and now?'"

"Holy shit, Dom, that's insane."

"Yeah, I know. I took off at that point."

"Do you carry?" he asked.

"I do, but I'm not starting a gunfight at a gas station in the middle of Austin."

"No, of course not. Did you get his license plate?"

"I was too panicked, to be honest. It didn't even cross my mind. It's just a red Honda Civic, maybe mid '90s."

He nodded. "OK. Type out a statement for me, exactly what happened. I'll start a report. And you better tell your boss, too."

"Oh, yeah." I'd not thought of that, how public this might become. But he was right, I'd have to say something. I stopped by Terri's office on the way to mine, her cheery smile dissolving as I told her what I'd told Trejo.

When I finished the story, she asked: "You don't recognize him?"

"Nope."

"I'll have to pass this up the chain, there'll need to be an investigation."

Which I didn't need. I said, "You know, being completely honest, I feel like maybe this was a road-rage-type thing."

"Did you cut him off or something?"

"I don't think so, but then if I had I would've done it by accident. Maybe I did and didn't notice. Anyway, I don't think we need the whole DA's office in a tizzy over this," I said reassuringly. "Certainly not yet, especially since I didn't recognize the guy." She frowned, so I continued. "Let's do this. I'll write a statement in case it turns out to be something, give it to Trejo, who's creating a report."

"That's good," she said.

"Yeah. And I'll just keep my eyes open for the dude for the next couple of days. If I see him, I'll call 911 and we'll know it's a thing. If not, then we'll know it wasn't."

"Are you sure? We could pull surveillance from the gas station, maybe get a plate and find out who he is. Send someone to talk to him."

And fuck up my plan. No thanks.

"No, thanks," I said. "That's a waste of resources at this point, really." I acted a little irritated. "I don't want this to be a big thing, Terri, I can look after myself without deputies chasing down every guy who doesn't like the way I drive."

"OK, OK." She held up her hands in surrender. "We'll stand down for now, if that's what you want." She wagged a reproving finger at me. "But if you see that guy again, if he follows you, then call 911 and we'll send the cavalry."

I gave her the thumbs-up. "That's a deal."

Phase One, complete.

CHAPTER NINETEEN

BRIAN

Dominic hadn't mentioned until now the treasure-hunt aspect to the poker game, but since it was pretty close to my apartment, I didn't mind. I think sometimes he gets people to do things just to amuse himself, like a power trip or something, but I wasn't sure in this case so I played along.

What Dominic didn't know was that I was getting ready for that poker night. I hadn't lied about not playing for a year or so, that was absolutely true. But I didn't see any harm in boning up a little. I bought a book on poker strategy and DVR'd a few of those Vegas competitions, not just watching the plays but also listening to the commentary, which was very enlightening. Connie didn't approve of poker, kept pushing me for details, but I sure as hell didn't dare tell her how much money was at stake. And once she understood that I was playing no matter what, she grudgingly let me do my research.

At six, I told Connie I was going to Whole Foods to get éclairs, her favorite. She's so easy to manipulate sometimes, I actually felt a little bad. But it was exciting, too, this almost childlike game I was playing with Dom and his friends.

I tried the apartment complex first, aware of my shiny, new Lexus as I cruised past all those crappy Chevys and Ford trucks. I didn't see a red Honda Civic where Dom said it might be. I was actually a little surprised that he'd know or be friends with someone who lived here; it's not a place you'd expect a cool, English musician-prosecutor to hang out. Maybe it was a friend going through hard times? Either way, I drove out of the complex breathing a sigh of relief, and headed to the library nearby. Sure enough, Dom's friend was parked in front of the building. I noticed that the Civic was in a handicapped spot. I'd not thought of Dom as the kind of person who had handicapped friends, either; seems like he wouldn't have the patience or sensitivity, or something. But then there was more to Dominic than I knew—there had to be, the way he was so good working with the kids at Gardner Betts, and the way he was being much friendlier to me.

I parked a dozen spaces away and watched for a moment. Dominic had explained that I'd be disqualified from the game if his mate saw me, and if challenged I had to play it off convincingly so that his friend didn't know it was part of the treasure hunt.

"Pretend you're at the wrong car," he'd said. "It's not that hard, he has no idea who you are or that you're coming to the game."

"What are the others doing?" I asked.

He gave me a look, like I was an idiot. "Dude, how can I tell you that? The way this works, I won't even know."

"But what's in the envelope?" I turned it over in my hands. "Shouldn't I at least know that?"

"You're not much of a rule follower, are you?" He seemed amused now.

"I am, I totally am. I just figured . . . I don't know how it all works, I guess."

"It's grown men playing elaborate yet childish games," he said. "Silly, pointless fun that we haven't gotten to do since we were kids."

"I can get on board with that," I said. "Six p.m., you said?"

"Right. Either outside his apartment, or at the library. And remember—"

"I know, don't get caught. Don't worry, I won't."

That's why I sat in the car as the sky darkened, watching. But I couldn't wait too long; Connie would be suspicious if I took forever out here. I opened my car door and picked up the envelope from the seat beside me. I started toward the library, strolling as nonchalantly as I could, but I stopped in my tracks when the front doors slid open. A woman with a stroller came out, and I breathed a sigh of relief. I started forward again, reaching the red Civic without incident. I stuck the envelope under a windshield wiper as instructed, then hurried back to my car. I sat in the driver's seat and watched for a few minutes to see if he came out. Now that I was safe, curiosity had replaced my nerves and I wanted to see who he was. But after five minutes I had to get going, so I started the engine and pointed my car north for my next mission: a quick trip to Whole Foods to find a succulent éclair to appease my girlfriend and nail down my alibi.

CHAPTER TWENTY

DOMINIC

I'd left half a dozen messages for her. She was trying to put distance between us, I knew, but I didn't like it because it was the wrong way around. She wasn't like the other women I'd dated, used, but even so her gapping me was the wrong way around. She finally called me at six in the morning and asked to meet for breakfast. A cold feeling settled into my stomach because this is what I did, how I ended things. A public place, a hangdog expression, and some variation of *I'm just not looking for a relationship right now*. Leave a fifty on the table to cover her breakfast, and send over a second cup of coffee for her to cry into on my way out the door.

Surely not. For me this was going to be a reconnection, not rejection. I thought hard about why she might be so adamant, and the only thing I could come up with was Bobby. With him gone, she didn't need me anymore. But really? Was it possible that everything else I had going for me held no interest for her?

Or maybe I was overthinking things and she just wanted to talk.

We met at Magnolia Grill, and she was already in a booth in the corner. She'd ordered coffee for us both.

No way.

I slid in opposite her. "You breaking up with me?"

"I think I did that already." She gave me that unreadable smile. "So what's to break up?"

"A beautiful thing?" I said it lightly, wondering what I'd see in her eyes. But she'd never been susceptible to that kind of charm, the glib and witty kind that worked so well on others.

"Sergeant Brannon called me again."

That took the smile off my face. "Why?"

"I don't know. He acted like he was checking in, trying to give me a chance to tell him something or other that I'd forgotten to mention before."

"And did you?"

"What do you think?" She dragged a few strands of hair across her face and twisted them in her fingers.

"I think you did not."

"Correct. Hopefully that'll be it. Dominic, I don't want him finding out about your connection to Bobby. You should be worried about that, too."

"I am, in my own special way."

A smile twitched her lips. "Your inability to worry might be your undoing one day."

I mock gasped. "Are you threatening me?"

"I don't need to, Englishman." She shook her head. "You threaten yourself every day."

Sad, but true. I paused for a moment, then asked, "Did they release his body yet?"

"Not yet. In a day or two, they said. I guess with homicides they're slower."

"They usually are, yes. I guess I can't come to the funeral."

"I guess not. Seems like they wouldn't really be your thing, anyway."

"True." I didn't want to say more, I didn't want to anger or alienate her, but then I also didn't want her calling things off.

"As I told you before, we shouldn't see or talk to each other for a while." She said it gently, as if I had feelings to hurt. "Which means you need to stop calling me."

"You think we're not smart enough to get away with seeing each other?"

"I think people overestimate how smart they are every day. And, personally, I think the smart move is to minimize our risk."

"Funny, from the one who started this whole ball of wax rolling down the hill."

She arched one eyebrow. "I don't think that's a saying."

"Whatever."

A plump waitress in a frilly dress and Doc Martins approached, pad in hand. "Y'all ready to order?"

I wanted to ask if her accent was real or put on for the tourists, but she looked like a delicate soul who might cry, and that'd make me look bad.

"Short stack with bacon, please," I said. "And I'm guessing an egg-white omelet with spinach and mushrooms, for the lady."

She nodded over her coffee cup, and the waitress trundled off.

"See, how cute that I can order for you."

She pursed her lips as she thought for a moment. "Look, I'm not doing this just for me; it's for you. Bobby's beyond getting in trouble now, but your old friend Tristan Bell is still trying to drop you in the grease; and if that cop finds out about us, he can draw a line straight from you to Ledsome's murder. He already has his motive, just waiting to kick in."

"I'm taking care of that problem," I said.

"How?"

"It's complicated."

"It always is with you," she said. As ever, her voice remained soft, like she was making an idle comment about the weather. "Things with you are either supremely complicated or incredibly simple."

"You think it's my fault I see the world the way I do?"

"No, of course not. People are responsible for the way they act, not the way they feel."

"You should be a shrink."

"And you'd be my first client."

"I'm beyond redemption," I said. "Ain't no fixing me."

She stirred her coffee. "I thought it was only stupid that couldn't be fixed."

"That, and me."

"We can't see each other again, Dom."

"This is really about keeping Brannon out of our hair?"

"Yes. Like I said, if he finds out about us, he's going turn up the heat, not back off."

"And it's not because you're seeing someone else?" I knew she'd been seeing one other lady, which I was cool with. Another guy, not so much.

"It's not. It's about keeping that one little secret."

"Big secret," I conceded.

"Right. Very big."

I looked at her for a moment, considering all the options. She was so beautiful, so poised, so assured, I knew that men everywhere threw themselves at her just as I'd done. But she was right about our relationship being the way we could be undone.

"It's funny," I said. "Me, you, and Bobby were the only ones to know about us." She waited for me to go on. "You know what they say, don't you?"

"What's that?" she cocked her head, watching me.

"That three can keep a secret." I smiled. "You know the rest of the saying?"

She nodded, not taking her eyes from mine as she spoke, her voice husky and low. "Three can keep a secret, when two of them are dead."

I started to say something, but she picked up her purse and slid her legs out from under the table. "Good-bye, Dominic."

I watched her leave, fishing around for an emotion but coming up empty, my eyes glued to that wonderful form, the gentle sway of her hips and the straightness of her back as she drifted between the other tables and out of the door. I stared in that direction until the waitress appeared in front of me, coffeepot in hand.

"A top-up, hun?" she asked.

I held out my cup, and that's when I noticed the twenty-dollar bill sitting on the table in front of me.

I smiled. "Yes. Thank you so much."

CHAPTER TWENTY-ONE

I left Magnolia Grill at eight, with a to-go coffee and the waitress's phone number. Depending on how things went, I might have time for her on the weekend. Something quiet at my place. She was a one-weekender at most, this one. I didn't mind the girth in the least; it was the cheesy Southern accent. If it turned out to be real, then she wouldn't even last a weekend.

I drove a slow loop to work, turned right onto South Congress, right again onto Oltorf, and then left on South First. The restaurant was all of two minutes from work but in the wrong direction for my new friend to be able to latch onto me, which he did as I passed the McDonalds where South Congress met US-290.

Technology lets you do wonderful things these days. In this case, track Travis Lee White on my cell phone to McDonalds and then drive slowly in front of him as he waited to turn onto Congress. A little luck with the timing, but that's fine with me. And once in position, there was no way he could miss me, the window of my white Land Rover down and music blaring, the hood of my car close to the bumper of the vehicle in front so White couldn't nudge his way in. That was bound to annoy him, which was very much my desire.

He had to wait for the car behind me to go, but then he bullied himself into the slow-moving line of traffic, earning himself an outraged honk from someone. I toyed with the idea of letting him know that I was aware of him being there, but decided to wait. We shuffled along for a mile, me signaling way in advance of the right turn onto Long Bow Lane. He turned right behind me, and I slowed so he'd know I'd spotted him, that large figure stuffed into a little red car, an angry man on the verge of getting his revenge.

I slowed a little more, just to irritate him, then stepped on the gas and roared the hundred yards to the parking lot in front of Gardner Betts. He obviously had no idea who I was or where I worked, because he bumped into the lot right behind me, our tires squealing. As the front of my car pointed toward the entrance, I flashed my lights as if I were afraid, knowing Deputy Trejo would be facing this way.

Trejo was out of the door a moment later, just as my car was diving into its parking spot. I leapt out and stared at the red Civic, which had stopped directly behind my car to block me in. Travis White glared through the window for a moment, anger and triumph on his face as he reached for the door handle. But Trejo was at the bottom of the steps and must have entered White's field of vision—a tough-looking deputy with his hand on his gun, about the last thing an ex-con needed in his life. White looked back at me with hatred, and with another squeal of tires he took off, that little engine screaming as he flew out of the parking lot onto Long Bow, and away.

Trejo was panting when he got to me. "What was that about? That him?"

"He followed me," I said. "He must have. I didn't see him until I turned into the parking lot—he just appeared out of nowhere."

He reached for the radio mic on his shoulder. "I'll call it in."

"Wait," I said.

He paused. "What? We need to hurry."

"But what are you calling in? I hate to be the one to say this, but he's not broken any laws."

Trejo looked at me. "He threatened you yesterday."

"Not enough," I said. "I don't think it meets the elements of ter-roristic threat, and he's not done enough to arrest for stalking."

"Yet."

"True, but until he does, there's not much we can do. I guess I'll write another statement, and you can supplement your report." I shrugged. "We can start there."

He nodded. "Let's get inside, though, just in case he comes back. And I got a partial plate, maybe we can do something with that."

"Just a partial?" I joked gently. "What kind of cop are you?"

"Yeah, I know." He looked sheepish. "But honestly, when I saw you flashing your lights, I thought the guy was about to shoot you or something. I kept my eyes on him for any kind of movement; I was way more worried about that than getting his plate."

"Well, I'm grateful, so no worries." I patted him on the shoulder as we made our way up the stairs to the entrance. "You reacted quickly, Mike, I'm impressed. I appreciate it, very much, looking out for me like that."

He held the door for me and smiled. "Just doing my job, Counselor."

O

When I first got to Maidstone Hall Preparatory School at the age of ten, there was a lot I didn't understand, but there were a few hurdles I didn't have to clear that others did. For example, a lot of kids found themselves surprised and upset that their parents would leave them alone at a school in the Scottish Highlands for weeks on end, with zero communication. Those kids had to persuade themselves it had nothing to do with how much they were loved or wanted at home. For so many in the upper echelons of English high society, tradition and a well-named school mattered more than seeing your own son or daughter grow up at home. That's easier for an adult to understand than a child.

Not an issue for me. When I watched my mum and dad drive away from Maidstone the first time, I knew why I was there. I knew that they loved me in the sense that they had to, biologically. I was also aware that family tradition meant I had to do my time at a character-building prep school, followed by a slightly closer-to-home boarding school until I was eighteen. But as I well knew, tradition was the rationalization, not the reason: a steady buildup of incidents around the family farm that had no good explanations—dead animals, broken equipment, small fires. . . . Those kinds of incidents.

The adjustment for me wasn't to the living conditions; I was used to the countryside and liked the remoteness of the place, especially the stress and loneliness it put on my classmates. I enjoyed those things, and could use them. No, the problem I had was with the idiotic conventions of the school, the customs that had been in place for a hundred years that made no sense to a boy for whom mere tradition was as idiotic as the prayers we said every morning.

For example, mischief was expected; after all, we were ninety or so kids living on top of each other. Nevertheless, there was this code of honesty such that whenever someone played a prank or broke something, caused a fight or stole someone else's candy, and they were confronted with it, they owned up. Without hesitation. That's right, the offender was expected not just to incriminate himself when questioned, but to confess immediately. I couldn't believe my eyes the first few times I saw it; it made no sense that you'd mess with someone or steal something, and then throw yourself to the wolves the first time someone in authority looked at you suspiciously.

To begin with I struggled over how to handle this. I didn't want to make myself an outcast by eschewing the tradition that would brand me as dishonest and a coward. Yet, nor did I have any desire to take responsibility, or do penance for, my misdeeds. But then I figured it out: all I had to do was pull my little pranks with someone by my side.

Then, when the time came for reckoning, I'd make myself scarce until my friend had raised his hand in a mea culpa. That way the masters would get their justice, my friend would be the honorable schoolboy by taking his punishment (and mine), and he could also feel noble at not turning me in. No point in both of us getting in trouble, eh?

After I ran away, right before my twelfth birthday, this became even less of a problem since the boys and teachers all felt the need to treat me with kid gloves. All except that one, Matthew MacIntosh, the oversized bully who hadn't gotten the memo about my untouchability.

He was a tall kid, soft in the middle, with thick red lips and dark wavy hair. I thought he looked like an ugly, fat girl, but I knew better than to say anything like that. I was athletic, slim and fast, and I could've eluded him in the open, but our simmering distaste for each other came to a head one winter Thursday in the main hall.

Another one of those stupid traditions I didn't get: at six thirty on weekdays, after the evening meal, we had thirty minutes of free time before reporting to our classrooms for prep. For those minutes the entire teaching staff would withdraw from the main hall and boys would "rag." I never knew if there were rules to this, because I never took part. I had no desire to wrestle with my classmates, particularly since the older boys tended to select the younger ones to pin in the dusty corners.

My usual plan was to step past the huffing and writhing mounds of schoolboys on my way to the table-tennis room, where I'd either play or pretend to watch those playing. Kids would occasionally ask me to rag, and I'd always tell them, "Next time" or say that I had a table-tennis match waiting. Matthew MacIntosh was particularly pushy, and particularly unhappy at taking no for an answer.

He was also very unhappy indeed at my newfound celebrity status.

"Hey, farm boy." He stopped me at the entrance to the hall just as the first tussles were breaking out. "How about it?"

"How about what?"

"You know. Rag."

I eyed the tumbling forms on the ground. "Seems a little gay to me."

"Bull. You're just scared."

"Of being gay?"

He pushed my shoulder. "Come on. Five minutes. If you cry, I'll stop."

"You ever seen me cry, MacIntosh?"

He sneered. "Not yet."

I leaned in, and his eyes widened with surprise. "I'm going to say this one time, Mac. I don't want to rag you. Not now, not ever. And if you try to make me, if you put your fat, sweaty hands on me ever again, I will make sure it's you crying on the floor, and everyone in the school will know about it."

I could see him gathering himself. I'd bet that no one had spoken to him like that in years, including his overindulgent parents. The cogs were spinning inside that thick skull, making it clear that he had a decision to make. And that he had two clear choices. His eyes slid left and right to see if anyone was watching, if anyone was close enough to have overheard my threat, close enough to watch him give in to it. His problem was that the answer was unclear, he simply couldn't be sure, and that made up his mind for him. He was all in.

His face reddened, and he pushed my shoulder with his right hand again. "You don't threaten me, you little pip-squeak."

"Mac, I'm just saying . . ."

"We're gonna rag right here and now," he growled, confident again.

I stepped into him again and felt his hot breath in my face. I put my nose against his and said, "No, we're not." He couldn't see my right hand balled up, had no idea it was headed straight for his gut, but his eyes widened the second it landed. I left my fist in there as he doubled over and sank to his knees, slack jaw gasping for breath. Ragging was wrestling, nothing more. No kicking, punching, or even pinching; just good clean wrestling.

Only, as usual, I didn't fight clean, wasn't playing by the rules, something Mac would've known if he'd paid any attention to me other than wanting to bring me down a notch.

He puffed and panted on his knees, then started to straighten up. I put my left arm onto his shoulder as if I were engaging him, playing his stupid game, and then I hit him again in the same place and he doubled over again, his forehead bouncing off the floor as he gasped for air. I rolled him onto his side so I could see the tears in his eyes, and then I leaned over and whispered in his ear.

"Everyone's watching you cry, Mac. I told you to leave me alone, and now everyone's watching you cry. If you come within three feet of me from now until I leave school, I will tell people that not only did you cry when we ragged, but that I'm pretty sure I smelled piss coming out of you."

"You bloody..." he stammered, but his voice cracked and he couldn't finish his sentence, maybe didn't dare to.

He crawled away from me and collapsed in a corner with both arms across his gut. I left him sitting against the wall, his puffy face frowning at anyone who dared look at him too long, one arm casually brushing away the tears with his sleeve when he thought no one was watching.

An early lesson for me, that incident. Two lessons, really. First, it pays to ignore the rules of the game sometimes, when those rules are stupid and liable to get you hurt. Second, if you're going to ignore the rules, then it pays to strike first, and strike hard.

CHAPTER TWENTY-TWO

I was pretty sure Travis White would recognize my car while I was out and about in Austin, and quite possibly keep an eye out for it. I considered leasing something more invisible, but quite frankly I enjoyed the thrill of maybe running into the guy before I meant to. As careful as I was being, I had to allow myself a little risk taking here and there.

My next step, on Saturday morning, was to go to the George-town Gun Show, a three-week-long display of deadly firepower at a conference center just north of Austin. It was like Ikea for weaponry. I'd been the previous year and been blown away, pun intended, by the range and number of weapons available for purchase. The prices were a little higher than I paid at the GT Distributors in town, a place that only sold firearms to law enforcement and at a discount, but a gun show had one major advantage: I could buy anything I wanted, and as long as I used cash there'd be no record.

But then on the drive up I-35 I started thinking about security cameras.

I often did this—flipping between reckless self-endangerment and excessive self-preservation. While it was true the gun couldn't be traced to me after a cash transaction, I wasn't sure if a serial number or something let the gun be traced to the dealer who sold it. In which case, there was an outside chance they look at security footage and somehow put me at the place where it was sold. And spot my white Land Rover.

I pulled over at a Torchy's Tacos and went inside. I ordered the Brushfire, my favorite, and a bowl of their refried black beans.

I was almost through my early lunch when I pulled out my phone and called for an Uber ride. I followed the driver's progress up the freeway, stopping and starting with the traffic on that bitch of a highway, and was waiting when he pulled up in his Chevy Malibu.

He wound the window down. "Hi. You call for an Uber?"

"Sure did," I said.

"Your name?"

"Dominic."

"OK, cool, hop in." Once I was in the front seat, he checked his mirror and pulled away. "Sorry, sometimes people pretend to be the person who called so they can get a free ride. I've taken to asking the person their name to confirm I have the right guy. Three or four times I've ended up giving some jackass a free ride just to avoid trouble. I'm Max, by the way."

"Nice to meet you, Max. You can't trust anyone these days, can you?"

"Too right. So, cool accent, where from?"

"Have a guess," I said.

"I'm thinking Australia."

"You ever been there?"

"No, always wanted to go," he said, his head bobbing enthusiastically.

"I'm from Sydney, born in the shadow of the Opera House."

"Oh, cool. They have a famous opera house, then?"

"That's why I mentioned it."

He turned a little red and I smiled. "Yeah, sorry. Americans aren't great with foreign geography."

"Or incredibly famous landmarks," I needled him. "But no worries, mate, no reason you should know."

"I'm a computer sciences student," he said, unasked, as he nudged the car into traffic on I-35. "Oh, we're going to the George-town Convention Center, right?"

"We are."

"What's going on there today?"

I wanted to lie, to keep messing with him, but he'd see for himself soon enough. "A gun show."

"Never been to one of those."

"Me neither," I said. "I'm at a loose end today, and I'm kind of fascinated by American gun culture, so I thought I'd take a look."

"You don't have many guns in Australia?"

"The Aboriginals are allowed to carry them, but no one else."

"Oh, man, really? You don't have any Second Amendment or anything?"

"Nah, we don't have any amendments."

"That must be weird."

No weirder than this conversation, I thought. "Yeah. Very."

We made it to the convention center without too much more idiocy, apart from the "G'day mate," he threw me as I got out.

Inside I recognized the familiar competing smells of gun oil and body odor. I drifted through the main hall, trying to avoid pockets of the latter in favor of the former. I stopped in front of stalls and chatted with the sellers, listening to their excitement about this weapon or that.

I think it's a true statement that the vast majority of English people, heck the vast majority of non-Americans, completely fail to understand or appreciate the gun culture in Texas and beyond. But I get it completely, and utterly love it.

That should make sense, too, because a gun is a lot like me. It's attractive and dangerous, thrilling and scary. A gun can go off by accident and cause no harm, or the ultimate harm. A gun doesn't care who it kills, or why; and a miss is the same as a kill, which is no different to a gun than a wounding. A cop and a criminal can use the same weapon for entirely opposite reasons, and the gun will work just the same for both.

Well, maybe there are a few differences: I care who tries to use me, and I care when I miss.

Once I was satisfied there were no cameras in the place, I made my purchase in cash and returned to the entrance of the center. I pulled up my Uber app and set my pickup location, relieved when Sandy in a minivan started my way. I didn't want another ride with that irritation called Max—if traffic was heavy and he was chatty again, my new gun might get a workout before I wanted it to.

Luckily, Sandy was the quiet type with no interest in talking to me about Australia, guns, or anything else. She and her thick glasses were focused entirely on the road, and for that I was grateful.

Once I was back in my car, I called Brian.

My phone rang just as I'd settled on the couch to watch a movie with Connie. It was Dominic.

"Hey man," he said. "You at home?"

"Yep, sure am. What's up?"

"Connie within earshot?"

I glanced over at her. "Sure is."

"You might want to take this in another room, then."

"Why?"

"Trust me on this."

I gave her a shrug and stood. As I left the living room I glanced over my shoulder at Connie, who rolled her eyes and picked up a magazine to wait for me, the movie paused at the opening credits. I didn't react, just walked through the downstairs bedroom and into the bathroom, closing both doors along the way.

"Is everything OK?" I asked.

"Of course. Are you busy tonight?"

"Umm." I thought of Connie. "I don't know, why?"

"Looks like the game might be this evening; we're just finalizing the location."

"Oh, jeez, really? Tonight?"

"That's what I said. If you can't make it, let me know now so I can try to get someone to fill in."

"I'm not sure, Dom." I wanted to play, of course, had been preparing to, but it really wasn't fair to just abandon Connie with no advance warning. She'd see it that way, at least.

"I know it's short notice, but that's how it is with these games." He paused. "And, I don't mean to put pressure on you, Brian, I know things at home can get dicey, but the guys don't usually give someone a second shot if they pull out."

"Oh, shit. Really?"

"Yeah. I mean, unless you're on your way to the hospital or get arrested or something major. It's a priority for them, and while we sometimes make accommodations for long-time players, the chaps like it to be a priority for everyone, especially the new guy."

I could feel myself starting to sweat. I really wanted to play, something bad, but I was sick of dealing with Connie's drama every time I wanted to do something without her. I certainly couldn't tell her I was hanging out with Dominic tonight, because that was a double risk for me: she'd be mad I wanted to go out without her, and because she has a crush on him, she'd beg and whine to come along. Maybe that was my way out . . .

"So, do the other guys bring their wives or girlfriends?"

Again a silence, then I heard him take a deep breath. "Brian, I'm going to assume right now that you're trying to be funny."

Message received. "Totally. Jeez, I mean that's the whole point of these things, right? Guys' night out?"

"Thank you," he said. "For a moment I was truly worried about you. So, in or out?"

I had to be in. Sure, Connie would be mad, but then she'd get over it. It sounded like Dom's buddies wouldn't get over me not showing up, though, and I didn't want to be excluded before I even went once. No way.

"OK, sure, I'll be there. Where and when?"

Dom chuckled. "Good man. I don't know yet, as it happens, and won't know until you tell me."

"Huh? I'm not following."

"As part of our cloak-and-dagger fun, you'll receive a text from a phone number that you don't know. It'll be one of the guys. You'll forward that address to my phone by text. Then I'll do the same for one of the others."

"Sounds weird."

"Like I said, we enjoy the cloak-and-dagger."

I thought about it a moment and, even though I didn't fully get it, I liked being in on it. "Hey, no problem."

"Bring a flashlight and a six-pack," he said. "We usually find an abandoned house on the East Side and use that. Adds to the excitement."

"Oh, wow, I bet. You're not afraid of, like, being caught on a criminal trespass charge?"

"Not in the least. I said an *abandoned* house, which means there's no one to press charges."

"Good point. Yeah, I'm in, looking forward to it. Any particular kind of beer?"

"I don't think it'll matter in the slightest," he said. "Bring whatever kind you like."

"Cool. Hey, I got those drugs, too, for the Russian roulette thing. I should bring those, too, right?"

"Oh yes," Dom said. "Absolutely."

CHAPTER TWENTY-THREE

DOMINIC

I couldn't decide whether I wanted it on film. Like, caught by surveillance cameras. On the one hand, if all went according to plan, then no one could dispute my account of events. I also loved the idea of having something I could watch over and over, a perfectly executed plan that I could enjoy for years to come.

On the other hand, if something went sideways, I couldn't explain it away because it'd be right there, captured on film. Say he didn't react properly or I had to abort, then there'd be a permanent record that could sink me at some point in the future.

I also had to be careful with the timing because there'd be interviews and re-interviews, and lots of hanging about while patrol cops talked to detectives and more patrol cops went hunting for witnesses. Time was of the essence with this deal, and I couldn't afford to be twiddling my thumbs, stuck in one spot while the pieces were falling into place somewhere else.

I decided against a permanent record of this particular event. As much as I wanted to trust my plan to be perfect, it was reliant in part on other people's emotional reactions, and as a man with very limited emotional range, I couldn't be sure that I'd pushed all of the right buttons.

As it turned out, I had to follow him for an hour until the right moment came.

He parked his little red Civic in the main parking lot of Wal-Mart on Ben White Boulevard, a lot I knew didn't have cameras, because I'd prosecuted a murder and several armed robberies that took place here, and each time the cops had been frustrated by the lack of security. Time being short, I didn't wait for him to go inside, instead picking an empty space closer to the store than his. Circumstantial evidence that I got there before he did, because everyone always takes the closest spot, right?

He spotted me lounging against the front of my Land Rover, checking my phone for messages. When I looked up, he was making a beeline for me, already working himself into a frenzy. I put on my most innocent face in case the Indian lady and her three kids loading bags into a minivan one row over were watching.

"Hey, you," he shouted, still about thirty yards away.

They were watching now. "Me?" I looked around, like maybe he was taking to someone else.

"Yeah, fucking you." He weaved past a few bumpers and stood five yards from me, the Indian family to our left. "What the fuck are you playing at?"

"I'm just . . . nothing. Looking at my phone."

"You know who I am. You're the asshole who blocked me in, screwed with me at the gas station."

"I think you have the wrong person," I said. With the noise of passing cars, I hoped the lady couldn't hear any actual words, just see his determined anger.

"No, I know exactly who you are!" he shouted. I was happy for her to hear that bit.

I glanced over, and the woman was ushering her kids into the car, a worried expression on her face. I made a gentle motion with my hands, telling her to get out of here.

"Look, old chap," I said in my most reasonable voice. "There's been some misunderstanding." I stepped forward, making sure my car blocked anyone from seeing the gun appear in my hand. White's eyes grew large, and he went from red-faced to something much paler very quickly.

"What the hell is this?" he demanded.

Poor guy had no clue, absolutely none. And how could he, really? He was even less engaged in my little game than was the lowliest pawn in a game of chess. He was more like a piñata, hanging there all innocent and inanimate, waiting to be whacked to pieces.

His eyes almost spun with confusion when I asked, "Are you left- or right-handed?"

He didn't reply, just looked from the gun to my face and back again. The info from the jail said he was right-handed, but I wanted to be sure. "I won't ask you again, left- or right-handed?"

"Right."

"Thank you," I said. "Now, the only way you live is if you shout the name 'Tristan Bell.'"

"What?"

"You have three seconds to shout the name Tristan Bell as loudly as you can, or you die."

He took a deep breath, his eyes on the gun, and shouted those two words louder than I expected. *Thanks again*, I thought.

Then I waited a half second and shot him through the heart.

By the time he hit the ground, I was at his side, making sure he was dead and making sure, too, that no one was watching as I pulled on a skin-colored pair of cotton gloves and took a second gun from my pocket. I wrapped his dead right hand around it, squeezing his palm around the grip, and then placed it quietly on the ground. I peeled off the gloves and stuffed them into the exhaust pipe of an F-250 that was beside me.

Then I stood and staggered back, reaching for my phone in time to see other people edging our way, already on theirs.

When the first patrol car arrived, I was already on my knees, my fingers interlocked on top of my head, and the gun on the ground ten feet from me. Even so, the officer had his gun out, and he moved between me and Travis White. He got to White first, kicking the weapon away from the body before kneeling to feel for a pulse. Before standing, he said something into his radio, then he moved toward me, gun aimed at my chest. Then his hand wavered and the gun lowered a fraction.

"Shit, Dominic, is that you?"

It took me a moment to recognize him. "Hey, Thiago. Wish I could say it was nice to see you again." *Don't be too cool,* I reminded myself. *A normal person would be full of adrenaline, maybe some remorse, and definitely be afraid.*

"What happened? Wait, are you armed still? Did you shoot that guy?"

"I'm not armed. That's my gun on the ground. I shot him once after he pulled on me."

"OK. You can lower your hands, but sit tight until my backup gets here." He moved forward and slid the gun farther from me with his foot, then stepped back and spoke into his radio. I heard a string of APD codes, and then my name. He waited for a response, acknowledging it with, "Ten-four" at the end of the conversation. He lowered his gun all the way, but didn't holster it. "Normally I'd ask you a bunch of questions, but they're telling me to wait for the detective."

"Which one?" As if I couldn't guess.

"Homicide. Name of Brannon, I don't know him."

"I do," I said. "Nice guy."

Within a minute, four other patrol cars had surrounded us and a crowd was starting to gather and gawp at the dead Travis White. More cops would be here to keep them away, I knew, and to find witnesses. Which reminded me.

"Hey, Thiago. Did the Indian lady leave? She saw what happened. Green minivan, right over there." I gestured with my head.

"Yeah, she called the cops, and someone's talking to her."

"Good, thanks."

"Hey, I'm gonna put cuffs on you and let you sit in a car. More comfortable than kneeling there—these detectives sometimes take their sweet time."

"No problem at all, I appreciate the courtesy."

"Cuffs are policy until we figure it out," he began.

"Please, it's fine, you're just doing your job. Only hope not too many people are filming this." Which they would be.

He put the windows down, but I was still uncomfortable, those rear seats were made for people with short legs, and the seat itself was hard plastic. With my hands cinched behind my back, I cursed Brannon for taking his time.

When he finally showed, he stood over White's body, which had been extensively photographed by a Crime Scene tech, and stared. Then he came over to me, Thiago unlocking the door and opening it.

"You can swing your legs out," Brannon said. "Pretty tight in there."

"Thanks," I said, and did so.

"Sure. You're not hurt are you? Need an ambulance or anything?"

"No, I'm fine. He didn't . . . I'm fine."

"Good," he said. "So, first thing I have to do, as I'm sure you understand, is read you your rights. You're not under arrest, but I want to do this by the book, be extra cautious."

"As you should, it's fine."

"The in-car recording system should capture it, but I'll have you sign the card, too." He took a blue square the size of a postcard out of his pocket and read me my rights. Then he gestured for Thiago to undo my cuffs and handed me a pen. I signed on the dotted line. "OK," he went on. "I don't think we need you re-cuffed."

I gave him a weak smile. "I don't think so either. My legs are too shaky for me to run off; I'd fall over."

He nodded. "Well, best not to try, then. So what happened here?"

I told him about the run-ins with White, my initial sense that I was being followed, and then the incidents at the gas station and him chasing me into Gardner Betts. That would be on camera, I assured him, as well as being witnessed by Deputy Mike Trejo. Then I told him how White had approached me in the parking lot right there, got my attention with his gun, and then yelled at me that this was from Tristan Bell.

"So do you know this guy?" Brannon asked.

"No. Before all this, never seen him."

"If he's a friend of Bell, would you expect to know him?"

I shrugged. "I mean, maybe. I didn't think Tristan had many friends; he didn't really have anyone over to the apartment. Maybe he's a relative?"

"We'll check. So he pulled a gun on you. He pulled first."

"Yes, of course. I don't know why he took so long, I don't . . . I wondered if maybe it'd jammed, but I just grabbed mine and shot. I didn't even aim."

"How many times did you shoot?"

"Just once," I said. "I think just once, anyway. Now that you ask, I wouldn't want to swear to it, but . . . yeah, I think just the one time."

"So if this has something to do with Bell, some revenge hit or something, how would he know you'd be here?"

"I can only think he followed me." I pointed away from the store. "He came from over there. I parked closer to the store, so he must have followed me here from somewhere. Again."

"OK. Wait here a moment."

He went and spoke to a patrol officer I didn't know, nodding as he listened. Then he came back.

"Talk to the Indian lady, she saw him approach me," I said.

"That's what Officer Wynn was telling me. She didn't see the shooting, or him with a gun, because her view was blocked. But she heard him say Bell's name. Shout it." He pursed his lips as he thought. "OK, so this must have been quite a shock, do you want me to get a counselor down here?"

"No, thank you. A nice glass of Scotch will take care of things."

A half smile. "Yeah, I'm with you on that. I'm gonna let you get out of here, but we'll need a formal statement, maybe tomorrow. I can have one of my guys drive you home and another follow in your car, if you're not up for driving."

"No, no. That's OK. I'm alright, really. I appreciate it, though."

"OK. Here's my card; call me if anything occurs to you. Anything at all, and any time." He helped me to my feet. "We'll need to hang onto your gun until we finish the investigation."

"Of course. I don't want to be around guns right now anyway, not for a while."

"That reminds me. You have a CHL?"

"I do." I made my fingers tremble a little as they opened my wallet and pulled out my license to carry a concealed handgun. He took and inspected it.

"OK, thanks," he said. "I'm glad you're all right. Go home and take it easy for the rest of the night. Enjoy that Scotch."

"Thanks, I will."

Not exactly the truth. In fact, I wasn't planning on sipping Scotch or taking it easy.

CHAPTER TWENTY-FOUR

There was a moment of respite at my apartment. I sat on the couch with my guitar, idly strumming a song I'd written two years earlier, "One Flew Over the Eagle's Nest." It was kind of a tribute to the Eagles, sort of an imaginary scenario where I played with them. It had that bouncy, catchy, almost-country rhythm that the Eagles mastered, and a chorus that my own fans loved to sing along to.

Ironic, of course, that I switched out the word *Cuckoo*, which was how I saw myself sometimes. An imposter dropped into someone else's nest, not of my own free will but most definitely at the expense of some poor innocent. Not that Travis Lee White was necessarily an innocent. A petty criminal with an anger problem and a propensity for parking in spaces reserved for the disabled. If I was looking to rationalize his death, I suppose I could start with those things, but I really wasn't. I just didn't care that much. Technically, not at all.

At seven, my phone buzzed, an address and time appearing in a text.

I ran my fingers over the taught guitar strings for a moment longer, feeling them quiver and hum under my fingertips. Behind them, the strong neck of the fingerboard, the familiar bump of the frets. My comfort, my rosary. I laid it back in its case and closed it.

I went to the desk in the corner and opened a drawer, pulling out one of the burner phones I'd stashed there yesterday. I hesitated for a moment because I knew that after making this call, there was no going back. On the other hand there was no way I could go back anyway, not altogether, so I dialed the number, getting voicemail.

"It's Dominic. There's something you need to know related to Bobby's death—the truth. I'm going to text you something. I'll explain when we meet."

Then I packed a bag, sent the text, and went out to my car. I had just started the engine when my cell phone rang, reminding me that I wasn't supposed to have it with me. I answered when I saw the 974 prefix.

"This is Dominic."

"Hi, Dominic. Jeremy Brannon. You have a moment?"

No. "Yes, sure."

"Don't mean to bug you, but I wanted to pass on some information we got, let you know where things stand as of right now on your shooting outside Wal-Mart."

"Tell me it's a self-defense finding, sure." I put a little extra exasperation in my voice to be sure it made its way down the line to him.

"Oh, God yes, absolutely," he said. "I can't see this going any other way."

"So who the hell was that guy, anyway?"

"His name was Travis White. Mean anything to you?"

I allowed a suitably thoughtful pause. "Travis White, no. Means nothing."

"Figured, but that's why I'm calling. Turns out your theory about Tristan Bell still trying to implicate you, get back at you, was right."

"What do you mean?"

"Travis Lee White is a former cellmate of Bell."

I let that sink in. "Are you serious? They were prison cellies?"

"Not prison, no. They bunked together when Bell was being held at Del Valle, pretrial."

"That's unbelievable. But why come after me now?"

"We're not entirely sure. We assume they've been in touch but haven't had time to confirm that."

"Bell put out a hit on me?"

"That seems likely. I mean, I don't think White tried to kill you just because he and Bell were friends."

"I guess not, but how would Bell pay this guy? He's locked up."

"Again," Brannon said, "it's early days. Well, hours. So we're not sure yet of the details. But I'll be honest, I've seen hits for a thousand bucks, couple hundred even. People like White don't have high regard for human life, especially law enforcement, whereas they do have a great deal of respect for the dollar."

"My life's worth a couple hundred bucks?"

"To someone like White, I expect it is. We should know more in a day or two, though."

"Well, I appreciate the update," I said. "Oh, and if you call back and I don't answer, please don't worry about me. I've taken a sleeping pill and plan to be out until morning."

"Good idea," Brannon said. "Just don't drink too much whiskey along with that pill."

I laughed. "Thanks, I won't."

We rang off, and I went back into my apartment and dropped my cell phone in the drawer beside my bed, then returned to the car.

I drove slowly and carefully up to Oltorf, then into East Austin, past the strip malls and laundromats, the liquor stores and shack-like Mexican restaurants where the best food was to be found, if you weren't in law enforcement. I didn't use my GPS to guide me, unsure if those things left a record that could be mined by anyone at a later date. But I recognized the street from my last visit and drove slowly up and down, making sure it was all clear. Not for the first time, I wondered about having such a visible car. A white Land Rover here was like a red flag to a bull, except it'd be stolen or stripped down, not charged at. But it was a risk I had to take at this point.

After I'd parked, I let myself through the little gate and walked up to the rickety porch, hesitating as I looked up and down the street. All quiet, and not even eight p.m. By this time the old folks would be stuck in front of their televisions, and the empty, unwanted homes were several hours away from being usurped by junkies and the homeless.

I tried the door handle, but someone had put a new lock on it. I walked around to the right side of the house and used the heel of my shoe to break a window and clear the glass away. I stood quietly for five minutes, listening for a neighbor or the sound of sirens, before dropping my bag through the window and hoisting myself inside.

I looked around, but it all seemed familiar, the same. The same as when I'd come in here with Officer Thiago DeAraujo. The same, too, as when I'd come here a couple of days earlier with Bobby and shot him in the side of the head. I wiped the gun on his hands in case he was found quickly and someone tested for GSR, and staged his body behind that mattress in the living room. The most distasteful part, as you might imagine, was handling the mattress, even though I was wearing gloves.

I dug into my bag and brought out a box of candles; I didn't want us all operating by flashlight. I had an electric lantern, too, which I switched to high and put on the coffee table, after propping up its broken end on a low wooden chair. I took care setting up and lighting the candles, as an unexpected fire wouldn't help my cause at this point.

Brian was the first to arrive. I watched him park and re-park his car right outside the front of the house. I could see his fat head in the glow of his phone as, no doubt, he checked and rechecked the address that I'd texted him from a burner phone, and that he'd sent on to me. He eventually got out of his car, carrying a plastic shopping bag and a flashlight, and made his way nervously up to the front door. I walked over and unlocked it.

"Come on in," I said. "Don't hang about out there; it's not the greatest neighborhood."

"No kidding," He said, then shot me a suspicious look. "Where's everyone else?"

"Running politely late, I assume."

"But they're coming."

"Won't be much of a poker game if they don't." I gave him a reassuring grin. "But if not, maybe we can play Go Fish or something."

He sniffed the air. "What's that smell?"

"All kinds of things—I wouldn't know where to start," I said lightly. "And I don't think you really want to know."

"You're probably right." He held up his sack. "Got some beers in here, those pills, where should I put them?"

"On the floor." I looked out of the window and saw headlights coming down the street, slowing as they reached the house. "Ah, here we go."

Brian reached into his bag and pulled out a beer. "I figured Connie wouldn't let me drink that Guinness you got for me, so I hid it and figured I'd bring it here."

Perfect. "Perfect."

A door slammed outside, and Brian said, "That one of the guys?"

"More or less." I crossed to the front door and opened it, so she wouldn't have to wait.

Brian had perched on the edge of the sofa, but when he saw her breeze into the room, he started to rise. "Oh, I thought . . ." he looked at me, "I thought it was just—"

"Just the guys? I think we can call this a change of plan."

He tried to recover, from his surprise and blatant rudeness. "Hi,

I'm Brian." Then he looked harder at her. "Have we met before? You look familiar."

"This is my girlfriend," I said, then corrected myself when she turned her elegant neck to look at me. "Former girlfriend. Whatever. You'll know her as the sister to a young man named Bobby, the deceased juvenile found by me." I pointed through to the bedroom. "In there, as it happens."

"What are you doing, Dominic?" she asked, her voice detached. And she didn't wait for an answer, but drifted over to the bedroom door. She picked up a candle on the way and stood in the doorway, looking in. Then she turned to me, her eyes wide with understanding. "Oh, Dom. *You* did it, didn't you?"

I didn't say anything. I didn't think I needed to, not to her anyway.

"Did what?" Brian looked back and forth between us, utterly clueless as to what we were talking about and what was to happen. "Dom, what the hell's going on here? Are we playing poker or not?"

"Not tonight, Brian." I walked over and locked the front door, more a symbolic gesture than a measure of security—even Brian knew how to operate a dead bolt.

My girl and I locked eyes across the room, but I couldn't read her, as usual. She moved slowly toward me, Brian watching her like she was an ice dancer in a miniskirt.

"I want to hear you say it," she said. "I've never expected much truth from you, I've always known what you were, but I would like the truth. And from your lips."

"What I am," I said, "and also what Bobby was."

"Which made it OK?"

"Basically, yes. A year ago, one person knew what I was, and that person was me. Then you came along and somehow you knew. And then Bobby knew." I pulled a gun from under my jacket and let it hang by my side.

"Dominic, what the fuck is—?" McNulty started to rise again but I waved the gun, indicating he should sit down. He looked up at the composed woman standing at the other end of the sofa and seemed to draw some courage from her calmness. "If someone doesn't tell me what the fuck is going on, I'm calling the police."

"No," I said. "That'd be a really bad move on your part."

"Why? I haven't done anything wrong."

"You might think that, but the police will be reaching a different conclusion fairly soon."

She smiled then, a sad little smile. "Ah, of course. Three of us knew about you. Three can keep a secret . . ."

"When two of them are dead," I finished for her.

"You brought him here to kill me?" she asked, still calm. "I don't believe that."

"What?" Brian almost exploded out of his seat and was halfway across the room when I caught up to him. I grabbed him by the collar and stuck the gun under his chin.

"If you stand up one more fucking time, I will kill you on the spot. Do you understand me?"

He nodded, and I dragged him back to the sofa, throwing him down. A cloud of dust rose around his lumpy form, and he sneezed violently several times. I stepped back and let it settle around him.

"Since you're so insistent on your innocence, let me tell you a few things," I said to Brian, once he'd regained control of himself. "Sometime tomorrow, the police will find a piece of paper in the glove compartment belonging to a man who tried to kill me. A piece of paper that has my home address, signed with your initials. They'll also find a letter bearing your fingerprints directing a would-be assassin to my place of work."

"My prints?"

"Yep. They'll run them through AFIS, and, since we're both

county employees, our prints are on file. Yours will show up; mine will not."

The wheels were spinning madly in his head. "The note on the Civic?"

"Precisely."

"What if he . . . threw it away?"

"It won't matter. They'll see the library footage of you putting that note on his car. If they don't figure that out themselves, an anonymous call will point them in the right direction."

"An anonymous call?"

"I've been making a lot of those lately. Burner phones are heaven-sent for that purpose." He was shaking his head, his mouth gaping open and shut like a drowning fish. "Now then," I went on. "Where was I? Ah yes. Once they connect you with Travis White, they'll take a look at the shell casings they've no doubt found by now in his trunk."

"Shell casings?" Brian said meekly.

"Yeah. You know, the ones I swept up when we went to the range. Amazingly a few found their way into my pocket and then into his car. I assume you don't have your gun with you now?"

His eyes widened, again, and he shook his head. "No."

"Don't lie to me, Brian."

He swallowed. "It's in the car."

"Bad neighborhood, this one. Give her your keys and tell her where it is, exactly."

He fished the keys from his pocket and handed them over. "Glove compartment."

"Good," I said. "That makes things even better."

We waited in silence as that blindingly serene form glided out of the house to Brian's car, returning with his gun clasped to her chest. She gave it to me, and I put mine back in its holster.

"Like I said, this makes things even better. Not that I needed it. I'm certain that once you're in APD's sights, they'll have a look at your work computer. That'll be a gold mine, right there."

"My computer? I never did anything with it!"

"Oh, but you did, don't you remember? Right after Detective Ledsome was shot, you tried to download the offense report to see where the investigation was going."

"No, I did that for you," he insisted.

"I wasn't even in the office; how did you do that for me?"

"You called! The phone records will show you called."

I shook my head. "No, they won't. They'll show you got a call from a number that isn't mine. A phone that was found on the body of Travis Lee White, the man who tried to murder me earlier tonight. The man you paid to murder me."

"Me? What are you talking about?"

"Oh, and speaking of your computer they'll find the e-mail you sent to Bobby's probation officer asking to track his GPS. You should really have been more careful about leaving your workstation unsecure."

"You sent that from my computer?"

"And that PO called a cell phone that can't be traced to me, and that the police will therefore assume was yours." I smiled broadly. "My goodness, how I love burner phones."

"I can't believe this." His eyes glistened, like he was about to cry. "Why are you doing this?"

I carried on. "It'll be tough to put the pieces together for the police, I'll admit. And they'll probably end up with a few gaps; I couldn't do everything the way I wanted. But there'll be enough connections to keep them happy, like the two grand you were going to pay White for the job. A lot of money to take out of your account at once, don't you think? And I'm guessing when she's asked about it, dear little Connie will have no idea."

He glanced down at his sack, where no doubt his poker money sat, then looked back and forth between the two of us, then at the gun in my hand. "I don't understand any of this."

"You were a dick," I said. "Basically, you were a dick and you wouldn't stop being one. And because you were such a giant dick, I decided that you didn't deserve to be a judge. In fact, I decided that not only did you *not* deserve to be one, but that I should have that job instead. Except I wasn't going to get it, was I?"

He was shaking his head. "I don't—"

"No, you and everyone else told me I wasn't going to get it. I don't like people telling me what I can and can't do." I glanced at my lady. "Sound familiar?"

"Very," she said, her face expressionless.

"Anyway." I turned back to McNulty. "That blackmail idea, that was genius."

"Blackmail? I didn't blackmail anyone . . ." His voice tailed off, confusion writ large on his stupid face, but also tinged with guilt.

"Brian, come on. I've never, ever accused you of being a genius. I'm talking about *my* blackmail idea."

"Judge Portnoy?" he asked. Maybe he was getting there, slowly. "How could you know about that? I didn't tell you. Or anyone."

"I know, and I'm most disappointed in your discretion. Judge Portnoy, however, is under the impression that the envelope she received containing a policeman's body-cam footage came from you." I could see he wasn't there yet, so I continued. "One of my cleverer schemes. I made sure you were close to Portnoy's house by following your patrol car that night, then diverting off for a wee prang."

"Prang?"

"Yes. I clipped that old lady and then scared her enough so

she called you. Which put you and Officer Chipelo right where I needed you, for an anonymous call to someone breaking into Portnoy's house."

He was still working it all out, but to be fair it was kind of a complex deal. "But how did you know what they'd find?"

"Well, let's start with the fact that I knew they'd be wearing body cams, that's where I started. Next we go to the fact, one you couldn't possibly know, that my lady here was utterly devoted to saving her brother from himself. Not only did she seduce me to that effect, but she . . . Let's just say she got on Judge Portnoy's good side. Very good side."

He turned and looked up at her, the truth slowly dawning on him. "That was you in there?"

"I told you, she likes to fuck with authority. Brian, come on," I said. "You really think I could've pulled this off all by myself? I'm good, but not that good."

He stared at the floor. When he spoke, a note of triumph laced his tone. "But Versadex will show that it was you who downloaded that video. If I didn't and you did, there'll be a record of that."

"Well, you'd think so," I said soothingly. "It's kind of true that you didn't do anything, except drink the laxative-laced coffee I brought you at Curra's. A little childish, of course, but so funny to see you scurry to the toilet like a little boy about to shit himself. In so much of a hurry, in fact, that you didn't log out of your computer— left it ready and waiting for me."

More pieces fell into place. "You downloaded it from my account."

"Mine kept glitching, remember?"

"Bullshit." He was angry now, which pleased me. He looked up, holding my gaze for a change. "So is that true? All that stuff Bell was saying about you masterminding that heist. Those murders."

"What do you think?"

He looked away from me, around the room, and his body suddenly sagged back into the sofa. "Are you really going to shoot me?" His voice was weak.

"No. Actually, I'm not." My special lady gave me a look, and I walked over and handed her the gun. "Elizabeth. It's time to choose. Me or him."

CHAPTER TWENTY-FIVE

BRIAN

'd known. I swear to God I'd always known, from the moment he moved into my office and shook my hand for the first time.

And yet I still couldn't believe it.

Well, maybe I hadn't known he was *this* bad, this . . . *evil*. And the truth was, even in that moment, in that awful, rundown house, I still had a hard time believing my eyes. A gun? None of this made sense, Dominic pulling my own gun on me and then handing it to her?

I dragged my eyes from the boxy Glock, *my* boxy Glock, and looked at their faces instead, trying to understand. They were staring at each other, their eyes locked but their faces were unreadable. I shifted on the sofa, edged forward, and the smell of the place rolled over me, dust and trash, piss and damp. Dominic's eyes swiveled and locked onto me, so I stopped moving. The girl stared at him still, the gun hanging in her hand like she didn't even know it was there.

I did. I couldn't tear my eyes from it.

I forced myself to, though, made myself look at her face; and when I did, I wondered if she was waiting for him to say something. A flash of hope hit me like lightning—maybe she was waiting for him to crack a smile and laugh at me, tell me this was hazing for the new guy who came to play cards.

But that didn't happen, and, like lightning, the brightness of hope flashed for a split second before it disappeared, letting the darkness of my fear settle over me again, chill my blood and bones as I waited for the same thing she did. Only I didn't know what it was, or when it'd come. I wondered if she did.

Once before I'd felt like this. When I was nineteen, I lived in Omaha, and one Sunday morning I was driving to the mall to buy shoes when a car ran a stop sign and crashed into a police car in front of me. Right into the driver's side, and the bang was so loud that I thought it had shattered my windows as well. I watched it happen, knew what was coming two seconds before it came to pass, like a slow-motion rerun.

I heard myself shouting *No!* a waste of my breath. And right after the crash, when I'd fallen silent and both cars had come to rest, there was a moment of complete and utter silence. A moment of unreality, too, as my mind was still processing what had happened—the explosion from a normal drive into a horrific accident, processing even as I got out of my car and walked toward the wreck.

The first sound I heard was a crunching under my feet, and I looked down at the ground and chided myself for stepping on the broken glass, but for no specific reason, as if I was equally guilty of contaminating a crime scene and also jeopardizing the soles of my battered, old shoes. One seemed as real as the other, both more immediate and real than the tangle of metal I was heading toward. My phone was in my hand, but I hadn't called 911—part of me wanting to make sure I needed to, to see it with my own eyes before taking up the valuable time of the emergency services.

The truth of that accident hit me when I got to the police car and looked through the driver's side window that had disintegrated over the blue uniform inside. The police officer's head had flopped to the right, his cheek resting flat on his right shoulder in a way that made me copy him, cock my head sideways to make sure of what I was seeing.

Broken neck. Broken neck.

And then: *Dead.*

I felt that same way, sitting on the dusty sofa, seeing it all but not believing it, my mind searching for other explanations and rejecting the moments of callousness from Dominic that I'd seen over the past year, the coldness and cruelty that nudged out of him toward me like tentacles, that I'd ignored then and was terrified of now. Clues. Signals.

I waited for one of them to say something.

CHAPTER TWENTY-SIX

ELIZABETH

Dominic stood between me and Brian McNulty and finally said what I needed to hear. What I already knew:

"I did it."

His voice was soft, matter-of-fact. "I killed Bobby. He murdered a police officer after I told him not to. I told him what would happen, that he'd never get away with it. I did it because they were going to catch him; and when they did, I'd get in trouble—you would too—and it would be the end for him. For all of us."

Somewhere outside, a dog barked, and I glanced toward the window behind Dominic. It was a square of gray; spider webs, dust, and dirt blocked out the light, and I was suddenly aware of the smell of the place. Mold, stale alcohol, and something chemical. Burnt meth, maybe. And this was the place my little brother had died.

Had been murdered.

"How?" I asked, not sure I even wanted to know.

"He called one of my burners. He called to brag. I told him to meet me here, that he could hole up and I'd bring him some supplies while we figured things out. While the cops calmed down a little."

"And you shot him in cold blood?"

Dominic stared at me for a moment. He did that when he was deciding on a tone of voice, a look, or some other calculated, fake emotional signal to appease me. But when he spoke, it actually sounded like the truth.

"That's the only kind of blood I have," he said quietly.

"Was he scared?"

Dominic shook his head. "Not for a second. At first he didn't think I'd do it. By the time he realized I had no choice, he was . . ." He shrugged, then paused. "We don't really get scared. You know that."

"Yes. I know."

Behind Dominic, McNulty spoke, his voice cracking. "Wait. He killed that kid? He murdered your brother?"

The gun felt heavy in my hand, and I looked at Dominic without answering McNulty. "Why do you think I won't shoot you?"

He smiled, he actually smiled as he nodded toward McNulty. "Because then you'd be here alone with him. You'd also have a lot of explaining to do about all this, a lot more than if you walk out of here with me."

"You killed my brother. You were supposed to be the one looking out for him."

His eyes flashed angrily. *Finally some emotion, you bastard.* "I put my job on the line for that kid, and all I ever got in return was attitude. Which I don't give a damn about, not really. But when he threatens my whole existence by shooting a fucking cop, then my caretaker role is over. Once he did that, all bets were off. All of them." He took a breath. "Look, you and I both know how I am. But you have to understand; I didn't want him spending the rest of his life in prison. I knew that would break you."

I shook my head. "Except you don't care that much about me. About anyone."

"You're wrong," he said. "You think I'm incapable of love or caring; but that's not true. Maybe it's more of a need than anything else, maybe it's not what *you* feel for people, but whatever you want to call it, I feel it. And I've felt it for you from the first moment I saw you." When I didn't speak, he carried on. "But you're right if you're suggesting I mostly did it for selfish reasons."

"Because you wanted to keep yourself safe. You figured he'd give you up to save himself."

"Of course he would have. The same way I'd sacrifice anyone else to save myself. That's what we do."

I hesitated a moment, then said, "That makes me wonder. Three people knew your secret, Dom. One's dead and I'm the other one. The only one who isn't you."

"And yet it's you standing there with the gun." He took a step back.

"You *want* me to kill you?" I didn't know if he was playing games again, or if maybe he was serious. I tried not to think about what he'd done, to keep my anger over that in check—because there was another side to this. Truthfully, and I'd never let him know it, but Dominic had been just about the best thing that had ever happened to me. He'd made a drab, endless existence exciting. He'd been the only one to help with Bobby. He'd been an outlet for my own desires to lash out at society, a tool for me to use to get money and have some fun, to break free of my own life for a while.

And until now, I'd assumed it was all no-strings. Dominic wasn't the only one who had a hard time feeling for his fellow man. I'm no psychopath, but my childhood and, so far, adulthood have been devoid of love. Men always chased me, women, too; but it's an exhausting game when you're always the prey. I was tired of being chased, and these days I never let myself get caught.

I so rarely get to be the predator. With Dominic, as dangerous as he was, I felt like the struggle was more even. I didn't love him and he didn't love me, but we were fascinated by each other. I always knew about his emotional limitations, and I'd done enough reading to know that keeping him at arm's length, playing it cool, would leave me in charge. Or something close to it.

But what was he playing at this time? Some kind of trust game?

"Thing is," Dominic was saying. "Everything I've said here tonight is kind of a secret." He looked over his shoulder. "Right, Brian?"

I felt bad for McNulty, truly. But I also felt bad for people who hopped into a cage with a tiger and got eaten. Which is to say, I didn't feel very bad, and not for long. Brian had done that; he'd poked at and irritated a tiger, gloated at getting a job Dominic wanted. Someone that dense, that blind, you couldn't feel too sorry for them—they're really just proof that Darwin was right.

"I guess," McNulty said. He seemed relieved I was holding the gun, which meant he didn't know what Dom was getting at. I did.

"Doesn't that mean I have to shoot you both?" I said, giving Dom a slight smile.

"I don't think so," Dominic said. "Because I think we need to alter that saying."

"How so?"

"Three can keep a secret, when two of them are implicated. And . . ." He paused and smiled, too.

"And the other one is dead?" I finished for him.

He stepped aside, and I raised the gun. I sighted it in the middle of McNulty's chest as his mouth fell open and the color drained from his face. I stepped closer, the barrel six inches from his shirt, but he didn't move, forward or back.

And then the trigger gave away, and my ears rang with the explosion. At first I thought I'd missed. Then McNulty toppled to his right, his head hitting the armrest and his neck bending at an unnatural angle. His eyes stayed open, as if surprised by it all. Which, in truth, I was, too.

I looked at Dominic, who said, "I wasn't sure you'd do it."

I didn't answer. I couldn't; I'd just shot a man.

"Are you all right?" he asked quietly.

I took a calming breath and told him the truth. "I figured it was him or you," I said. "Maybe him or me."

Dominic smiled, but his eyes glittered in the candlelight. "Either way, better him than either of us."

"Yeah," I said, though I felt like my throat was closing up. "I guess so."

I realized I was still holding the gun up, as if McNulty might come back to life. Or as if my arm was in control, and not me. I lowered it and looked Dom in the eye. "I'm trusting you," I said. "I'm trusting you to have all this figured out."

"I do. Even if you'd shot me, he would've taken the blame and you'd be in the clear. You know, assuming you'd wiped the gun clean or handed it to him. Which reminds me." He went to his bag and took out a pair of latex gloves and pulled them on. Then he took out a cloth and walked over to me, putting his hand out for the gun. I gave it to him and watched as he wiped it down, his movements slow and careful, Dominic handling the gun like it was a baby and he was caring for it.

When he was done, he went over to McNulty's body and pressed the gun into his hand, making sure DNA and fingerprints were on it, I guessed. Then he dropped the weapon onto the floor and I flinched, but it didn't go off. Dominic laughed gently.

"They're made not to go off when you drop them."

"I didn't know that," I said. "Not a regular user of guns."

He inclined his head toward McNulty. "Could've fooled me."

I was glad he'd taken the gun away; my hands and fingers were trembling with the adrenaline, my heart still pounding. "He committed suicide?" I asked.

"He did."

I looked at the chest would. "Do men commit suicide that way? By shooting themselves in the chest?"

"Not usually. Usually the head, either under the chin or through the temple. Women usually do it that way, in the chest."

"For real?" I felt a sudden chill run down my spine.

"Preserve their beauty. That's the theory, anyway. In reality, the only women I've seen commit suicide that way didn't have a lot of beauty to preserve."

He was pulling cans out of his bag. "What are those?"

"Empty beer cans. Once they start putting two and two together, they may have another look at Bobby's death; I'm not sure." He went into the bedroom and tossed a few cans into an open closet. "They have McNulty's prints on them. I was going to use them at White's shooting but didn't have time to put any in his car. They can be insurance here, so to speak."

"Will they find evidence of us here?" I asked. "I didn't keep track of what I touched. Maybe DNA somehow?"

"I was here with the police, so if they find my prints or DNA it won't mean anything. And if worse comes to worst," he said, "you can tell them that you came by the house because it's where Bobby died. You can say that you wanted to see it. They won't be happy, but they'll understand."

"You really do think of everything, don't you?"

Except he didn't know how close he'd come to dying. He didn't know how strong the urge was for me to swing my arm six inches to the left and shoot him for killing Bobby, giving him the same ending in the same place—a poetic justice I have no idea whether he'd understand or not. I really had considered doing that, had to fight the urge to do it; but I knew he'd have thought of that, too. Even if he was telling the truth about his feelings for me, I knew somewhere in this complicated scheme there'd be a booby trap for me if I turned on him. Something of mine left somewhere the police would see it. A fingerprint, an e-mail, some sort of trail. And, as he'd told me so many times, once the police lock onto you, they keep going until they get you, unless you can prove to them you're innocent. That's what it takes, he says, that you have to prove your innocence to them. Backward, but that's how they do it. And impossible for me, obviously. First of all, if I shot him I wouldn't *be* innocent. Second, I have no idea what's been happening inside Dominic's mind for the past week. I have no idea why he lured McNulty here to kill him, for *me* to kill him. I just know, 100 percent know, that if Dominic didn't get his way today, then I'd be next for the firing squad.

And with Bobby gone there was no one else left in my life for me to protect, only myself and maybe a drug-addicted aunt.

Dominic left his gloves on as he gathered up Brian's bag, and he showed me the envelope full of cash. "Take it. I don't need money right now."

I did take it. It would pay for Bobby's funeral. But I didn't say thank you. "Should we put out the candles?" I asked.

"No. I expect the cops will be here before long; and if not we can call them ourselves. In the meantime, one of those candles might just topple over and start a nice little fire. Make sure our tracks are covered. Either way, we're good."

"You're sure?"

"You know I am." He straightened and smiled. "And I find that life is more fun when you leave a little something to chance."

CHAPTER TWENTY-SEVEN

DOMINIC

The news shows and papers were all over the story by that evening, and I could see why: a conspiracy and an attempt to kill one prosecutor, another dead prosecutor found in the same house where a cop-killer had shot himself in the head. It was like there'd been an old-fashioned Wild West shoot-out and the good guys had won. The next day, CNN, FOX News, and every major newspaper sent someone to Austin to cover the story. And everyone wanted to interview me. Twice in a year I'd been targeted, and twice I'd managed to escape with my life and my freedom. I was at the center of this story, and my phone didn't stop ringing until midnight, then started again at six the next morning.

I continued to play hard to get on Sunday. I didn't answer my phone unless I recognized the caller, and I didn't answer my door at all. All I did was announce on my website that I'd be making a statement after my Monday evening gig at Steamboat. I knew full well that the journalists would try to get a jump on each other to buff up their stories as much as possible with B-roll shots of me playing and, I'm sure they hoped, a private word, so I called Bernadette Phillips and told her to put out extra empty beer jugs that she used for tip jars. She laughed when I told her why, and we both knew I'd win our bet that night.

I did. Every journalist and thrill seeker in the place—and there were hundreds—made sure to catch my eye as they dropped fives and tens into the tip jugs. A couple of the early stories had compared my survival to that of a cat, perhaps thanks to my subtle suggestion via friends, so the cameras clicked and flashed when I started into one my own songs, "Nine Lives." You can't imagine the feeling of such an adoring, admiring crowd, a mass of people crammed together, spilling wine and beer on each other, and all thinking they were the only ones to make the connection. And all of them, every single one, dancing like my puppet to the song I knew I'd be playing for them.

At the end of my set, Bernadette paid up quickly and happily, as well she should have because I'd made her even more money than I'd made for myself, and she knew she had no cause for complaint. She'd even set aside a conference room on the second floor, and I fielded questions in my usual way, humble and respectful, sipping at my post-gig bottle of water as I said the right things and pulled the right faces: appropriately sad for the dead, duly modest about my role in defending myself, and suitably observant of the rights of those as-yet-unidentified people heading into the whirling blades of the justice system.

Throughout the gig and the press conference, my eyes drifted to two different people who stood at the back of the room, not near each other and acting like they weren't aware of each other. The place was so packed, maybe they weren't.

One was a beautiful woman, more beautiful than I'd ever seen, wearing for the first time in a year the lime green dress that showed off every brilliant curve and straight line she had, every dip and rise of that perfect body. She wore her red heels, too, drawing my eye and countless others to those taut calves, the start of an irresistible journey upward to her creamy complexion and those cherry red lips that barely moved as they silently mouthed the words to my songs. She was a siren-like seductress to me and everyone else there, perfectly gorgeous yet unattainable, her movie-star hair framing her face and glowing like burnished gold in every light that place threw at her.

The other figure at the back of the room was Sergeant Jeremy

Brannon, slouched in the corner, looking like a common PI in his trench coat and fedora, as if he were at a costume party playing a cheesy version of himself. He didn't sing along but, to his credit, he was the one who found me in the little kitchen behind the conference room after I'd slid the mic into its holder and politely, respectfully, and humbly excused myself from the media. He came in as I was refilling my water bottle from the tap.

"That won't be cold," he said.

"Doesn't matter. I'm just killing time until they clear out." I nodded to the door to indicate the journalists.

"Didn't take you for the shy kind. Then again, you never really know anyone, do you?"

"Meaning?"

"Great show, by the way, I've never heard your music but it was good. Really good."

"Thanks."

"Welcome," he said. "You know, I talked to him recently."

"Talked to who?"

"Brian McNulty. I met with him at your offices and thought he was kind of a wet fish. You know, not very bright, not very interesting. And then he does all this."

"All this?" I asked. "I guess I'm still not clear about exactly what he did." *Which is to say, what is it exactly that you think he did?*

"Well, it looks like he started by blackmailing Judge Portnoy."

"Are you serious?"

He gave me a look. "It's OK; I know you know. The judge came forward and did the right thing after we found his body. Phoned us Saturday night."

"I'm glad to hear that. I told her to report it in the first place, when she first came to me."

"We know, don't worry you didn't do anything wrong. And

I certainly don't blame her for trying to keep something like that secret; it's a normal human instinct."

"Yeah, I guess so."

"Anyway," Brannon continued. "We're still looking into the connection between him and Tristan Bell; I can't wait to find out how they hooked up."

"You're sure they did?"

"He took out two grand from his bank account. His girlfriend knew nothing about it."

"Sneaky bastard."

"Yeah. If I had to guess I'd say Bell and McNulty were friends back in the day and y'all just didn't know it, although it's possible they got to know each other after his arrest. People like Bell attract all kind of attention, from people you wouldn't believe. Anyway, Bell and White must've gotten cozy in jail, and Bell put him onto McNulty. Two thousand bucks is a lot of money for someone who's been in and out of jail for the past decade."

"I'm sure. But how would Tristan pay back Brian?"

"No idea. Maybe McNulty was already indebted to him; this was paying *him* back."

"I suppose that's possible. You said you don't know how he and White got together?"

"Not yet. I do know that they communicated via phone, no texts. We found a burner phone on White's body, a couple of calls had been made to it from the one we found on McNulty. Same make of phone, too, he probably bought a few of them to use."

"Sounds like it. So do you think McNulty killed himself?"

"We do. Once he heard that White was dead, he figured he'd finish the job himself—hence the text to you to meet him at that time and place. When you didn't show up, I can only assume he got to thinking and realized there was no way we wouldn't catch him."

"For the blackmail?"

"That and the conspiracy to kill you," Brannon said. "With White dead, McNulty would have known that we could go through White's stuff and find out why he was after you, who was helping him. Being a prosecutor, McNulty would've known how thorough we'd be and that we'd figure out his role. Like I say, he probably got to thinking about it when you didn't show up, and realized he was in a corner."

"Seems extreme to go from wanting to kill me to killing himself."

"Not really," Brannon shook his head. "Do you have any idea how a prosecutor would fair in prison? Let alone one with McNulty's personality and presence?"

"Good point." I wondered if he had a theory for why poor Brian might choose that location to kill me. *No harm in asking, right?* "Why there do you suppose?"

"I can only think he wanted an abandoned property far away from his place. I expect he heard about it from you, or someone else, talking about that kid being murdered there. We know he'd been there before, though, probably to scout the place."

How's that possible? "How do you know?"

"Beer cans. Some in the bedroom with his prints—we missed them first time we went through the house, just because we weren't really looking for anyone else."

"Beer cans?" If he bothered to test the liquid left inside those cans, he'd discover large doses of Flunitrazepam, also known as "roofies." Which might lead him to think Brian had dosed Bobby and brought him here to kill him. I was fine with the current working theory, though—no need to make things *too* complicated.

"Guinness, to be precise. Dutch courage. Probably drank them while picturing what he planned to do, help him get through it." Brannon shrugged. "That's just a guess, of course."

CHAPTER TWENTY-EIGHT

ELIZABETH

I don't know why I went to see Dominic perform that night at Club Steamboat. I think I wanted to throw him off a little, make some kind of power play. I dressed the way I had when I first caught his eye, and I lingered at the back of the room, watching him play the crowd like the puppets they were. Maybe that's it, I wanted him to know that in a world of puppets, I wasn't one of them.

If I had to guess, I'd say Sergeant Brannon wasn't either, but he did look defeated in his hat and cop coat. I thought about going over and talking to him, feeling him out a little, and I know he spent a fair amount of time looking my way. But that might have made Dominic mad, and if there was one lesson from the past year of my life I'd taken to heart, it was that making Dominic mad ended very, very badly for whoever had done so.

I didn't see Dominic again after that night. I noticed his picture in the paper two months later, shaking Judge Portnoy's hand as he was sworn in as the new Associate Juvenile Court Judge. Of course, I didn't see Barbara again, either. She was gun-shy, and since most of our relationship was based on me looking out for Bobby, I had no more reason to pursue her.

Not many people showed up to Bobby's funeral. A couple of his friends, his probation officer. The highlight was when members of two rival gangs ran into each other at the cemetery gates. That resulted in a lot of posturing and everyone walking away shouting insults. I suppose I should be grateful that there was no fight, that none of them came in.

Jeremy Brannon did, though. I wondered if he was waiting to see whether Dominic appeared, even though I knew that wasn't going to happen. After the brief service, Brannon came up to me and shook my hand.

"I'm sorry for your loss, truly," he said.

"Thank you." He held onto my hand just a moment too long, and it clicked as to why he was really there. "It's kind of you to come."

"Of course. Was it just the two of you?"

"Yes." I didn't feel like answering questions, and I should've been annoyed that he showed up to my brother's funeral to make a pass at me. At least he wasn't wearing a wedding ring; that made a nice change. In another time and place I might have thought of taking him on as a project. He was good-looking, had a decent job, and seemed nice, kind. But I liked to fuck with authority, not the other way around, and after my recent dalliances I was starting to think that "nice and kind" might become a little boring after a while. A very short while.

I thought about Brian McNulty quite a lot. About innocence and being in the wrong place at the wrong time. About luck. Specifically bad luck. Bobby had been unlucky with his genes. I guess Dominic was, too. Was I lucky he spotted me at the bus stop? No, that was by design. My design. So what was it that put him in my life for the past year? Good luck or bad? Good planning or bad?

The thing is, none of us is responsible for where we start in life. I can't help my emotional detachment, my shitty parents, my addict aunt. All I can do is try to improve my life, and while I tried to do that without stepping all over other people, I was starting to believe that maybe that was inevitable sometimes. I do know that I can't be responsible for saving the likes of Brian McNulty and, while it's true that I did a lot more than "not save" him, it's also true that I had to choose between his life and mine. Who in the world would have chosen differently?

That saying about three people keeping a secret turned out to be wrong, too. Dominic and I had all kinds of secrets going on, and we managed to keep them from the world. Add Barbara Portnoy to the mix, and you have to admit that three *can* keep a secret. Although I'm pretty sure Dominic will break that one out and use it against her if he needs to.

Sometimes I wonder if I'm worse than him, than Dominic. I prodded him to pull that heist, I used my body to control him, to control a district judge, and I killed someone. Yes, I can find excuses or reasons for all of it, rationalizations—but that just makes me like Dominic, thinking that the ends justify the means. And he has an excuse built in, a design flaw that I don't have. . . . That's why I wonder if I'm a worse person than he is.

I'm not, though, I know that. You see, I have the ability, the capability, to love someone else, to feel for others. That makes me different and, I hope, slightly better. Even if I don't always act right, there's hope for me; there's a chance that my life will straighten out and that I can put all of this behind me. Reinvent myself, you could say. That's what I thought about as I walked away from Bobby's funeral. That I had a chance to start afresh, and while I knew that it wasn't much of a chance, it *was* one, and it was there for me.

For Dominic, not so much.

CHAPTER TWENTY-NINE

DOMINIC

In the week after my gig at Steamboat, I spent a fair amount of time wondering why Elizabeth hadn't shot me instead of Brian, and I think it came down to one thing. Just one. I think that she knew, deep in her heart, that Bobby would have ended up behind bars for killing a cop and, on his way to prison, he'd have ruined her life and mine.

Even if she didn't care about me anymore, which I doubted, she's no different from me in that self-preservation is a priority, a reflex almost. Now, with Bobby gone, she was safe, and I was the one who'd made her safe. That's why she shot Brian instead of me: as weird as it sounds, she thought I'd done the right thing.

Put slightly differently, she let me live because she truly believed that Bobby was the one who'd killed Detective Ledsome.

ABOUT THE AUTHOR

Mark Pryor is the author of *Hollow Man*, which introduced the protagonist Dominic, and the Hugo Marston novels: *The Bookseller*, *The Crypt Thief*, *The Blood Promise*, *The Button Man*, *The Reluctant Matador*, *The Paris Librarian*, and *The Sorbonne Affair*. He has also published the true-crime book *As She Lay Sleeping*. A native of Hertfordshire, England, he is an assistant district attorney in Austin, Texas, where he lives with his wife and three children.